A DANCE IN THE OCEAN

A SAGA OF ROMANCE, DESIRE AND INTRICATE BALLET OF DESTINY

PRIYANKA GUPTA

Made with ♥ on the Notion Press Platform
www.notionpress.com

For those who believe in the power of a single touch, a lingering gaze, and the magic of two hearts entwined.

May it remind you that love is an exquisite tapestry woven with laughter, tears, and moments that take your breath away.

Contents

Prologue vii

1. ♥?One 1
2. ♥?Two 7
3. ♥?Three 15
4. ♥?Four 28
5. ♥?Five 35
6. ♥?Six 40
7. ♥?Seven 44
8. ♥?Eight 51
9. ♥?Nine 58
10. ♥Ten 62
11. ♥Eleven 66
12. ♥Twelve 77
13. ♥Thirteen 82
14. ♥Fourteen 86
15. ♥Fifteen 91
16. ♥Sixteen 96
17. ♥Seventeen 101
18. ♥Eighteen 107
19. ♥Nineteen 116
20. ♥Twenty 121
21. ♥ Twenty-One 130

Prologue

In the heart of the bustling city, where the ebb and flow of life creates a symphony of stories, two souls embarked on a journey that would forever alter the course of their lives. It was a tale of love, passion, and the intricate dance of fate.

She, Tara, a woman with a heart full of dreams, had always believed in the magic of love, while He, Neil, a man driven by ambition, had built walls around his emotions. Their paths crossed in the most unexpected of ways, a chance encounter that would set in motion a love story neither of them could have foreseen.

In the pages that follow, we invite you to join us on this enchanting voyage through the highs and lows of love, where secrets and desires lay hidden beneath the surface, waiting to be uncovered. Welcome to a world where the heart's whispers are as powerful as the roar of the ocean, and where love can rewrite the destiny of even the most guarded souls.

This is their story, a story of love, redemption, and the eternal quest for the one thing that binds us all-the promise of a love that transcends time and space.

Author's note

Dear reader,

I sincerely thank each of you for embarking on this romantic journey with me. It is a privilege and a pleasure to share this story with you all.

This novel occupies a special corner of my heart. It was conceived from a profound desire to unravel the complexities of love, to dive into the profound connections between people that leave us spellbound and irrevocably transformed.

This is a narrative laced with hushed vows, stolen gazes, and the tangible electricity that lingers in the atmosphere when two hearts intersect.

I would like to express my gratitude to everyone who played a role in shaping this story. It has been an exhilarating voyage, spanning from the conception of the idea in my mind to the moment I held the book.

And finally, I wish to Thank You, cherished reader. Your engagement and enthusiasm for this genre are the very embers that keep the fires of romance burning. I trust that the moments you share, while lost in these pages, will bring you happiness, inspiration, and unshakeable faith in the potency of love.

With love,
Priyanka

The phone tolls incessantly while a multitude of emails stream ceaselessly throughout each passing moment of the day.

Doubt hangs in the air, leaving one unsure where to begin unraveling the enigma behind the relentless decline of the company's shares.

In the span of the past half-century, it descends to its most abysmal record. Wadia Industries boasts an esteemed reputation amongst its peers and the market.

I observe the sense of urgency in every employee as they receive the news, all displaying visible signs of concern regarding this situation.

There are individuals attending to phone calls, while others are diligently handling the influx of emails.

My dedicated secretary, Ana, has been attempting to reach me for the past two hours, but I have been apprehensive about allowing her access to my presence.

In a whirlwind of urgency and unease, Ana rushed anxiously to my office, delivering news of utmost importance, "Sir, I must inform you that the highly anticipated board meeting is set to commence in a mere 10 minutes."

As a CEO in my early thirties and the sole owner of this vast empire, I carry the weight of numerous pressures and expectations.

Nevertheless, I take genuine pleasure in not only meeting but surpassing these demands. This dynamic challenge fuels my ambition and serves as a constant source of inspiration, driving me to strive for even greater heights.

The moment she departed, Kabir Ahuja, CFO of Wadia Industries, stormed into my office with an air of weight. "Dude, where have you been? I've been trying to reach you for what feels like an eternity! Listen, don't worry. We have always managed to find solutions. Just take a moment to relax."

Kabir and I have been inseparable friends for as long as I can remember. We were schoolmates and even attended Stanford together.

Upon returning to India, we made the joint decision to collaborate in revitalizing my father's business. Since those early days when we used to argue over candies, we have stood by each other through thick and thin, supporting each other unconditionally.

In my recollection, Kabir has consistently been the epitome of faith and support in my life. No matter the adversity or extremity we faced, he has always been the one to reassure me,

"Hey, everything is going to be alright. I am right here by your side."

From his perspective, I possess the ability to handle any situation with an endless supply of contingency plans. He possesses a confident assurance, believing that I am somewhat of a superhuman equipped with a magical wand, capable of solving any mystery in the blink of an eye.

As expected, he once again holds unwavering confidence and hope in my supposed magical powers, "I know you can do it. Just take a deep breath and instruct me on what needs to be arranged, who should be let go, and who we should bring on board."

I acknowledged him with a subtle nod as a response, urging him to calm down,

"Kabir, You need to take a deep breath and relax. There is no need to get panic, Everything is under control. Let's devise a plan on how to approach this situation. Meet me in the boardroom in 10 minutes."

Typically, these situations don't ruffle my feathers much, I tend to view them as an integral part of life's grand tapestry.

However, Kabir displays an incredibly strong sense of protectiveness when it comes to my emotions.

He's resolute in his determination to ensure that I remain unburdened by unnecessary worries. His unwavering commitment to my peace of mind in the face of life's challenges is both striking and profoundly reassuring.

I am now tasked with formulating a robust plan and strategy to substantiate that the situation is well-managed, with the imminent restoration of share prices on the horizon.

To quell my nerves, I consumed three glasses of water before making my way towards the boardroom.

"Good day, esteemed colleagues. Please take your seats. I am well aware that the current state of the market may seem challenging. However, I implore you all to maintain confidence in our system. Rest assured, we are actively addressing the decline in share prices and will regain control swiftly."

"At this crucial juncture, I humbly request your unwavering support, as you have shown in the past."

A sharp retort comes from a board member,

"I must express my skepticism, Mr Neil Wadia, regarding the promises you are making. I apologize, but I fail to see a clear plan on how we will stabilize the scenario."

"I value your honesty and understand your concerns. However, I can only urge you to trust the foundation we have built. I assure you that a comprehensive plan will be shared with you via email within the next 2 hours. Furthermore, I kindly ask that any investor concerns be directed to me for swift attention."

"I would like to express my sincere gratitude to all of you for attending this meeting at such short notice. Wishing you all a wonderful day." I concluded.

It's just Kabir and me left in the boardroom. Kabir paces back and forth, his hand resting on his forehead in deep thought.

"Neil, how can you make a promise to the board about sending a comprehensive plan within the next 2 hours? We must think fast and strategically. The situation is slipping out of our control." Kabir blurted out.

In a calm tone, I instructed, "Kabir, I need you to find me an exceptional marketing expert by tomorrow. Please filter out any candidates who are just standbys, and hire someone who excels in content creativity and strategic thinking."

Kabir still seemed hesitant and surprised, "Bro, you need to tell me what you're thinking. I can't see where you're going with this."

I tapped his shoulder, "Don't worry. Just trust me and do as I say."

As I returned to my cabin, I quickly drew the blinds. Immediately called Ana, "Hey, please redirect all calls and make sure nobody disturbs me."

"Also, kindly ask Ashok to leave for the day, I will call him when need him again."

"Sir, are you planning to stay overnight here?" Ana asked, surprised.

Ignoring her question, I proceeded, "Please ask Kabir to come to my cabin as soon as possible and send me the financial files for today."

Ana sounded slightly anxious to learn more, but I abruptly ended the call.

After approximately fifteen minutes, Kabir arrived. He still appeared nervous.

It is worth mentioning that Kabir's anxiety stems not only from the current situation but also from the fact that the entire scene is causing me stress.

"Neil, I think you should take a moment to catch your breath and have a cup of coffee.

"I get it, buddy. Rest assured, we'll have the situation well under control in no time. And as for me, there's no need to worry—I'm doing just fine. You know that I relish facing challenges like these." I expressed, releasing my emotions.

"Okay, I suppose you're right. Let's get to work," Kabir pulled up a chair and started to review the files.

Out of nowhere, he exclaimed, "Bro, I know this person who could be super useful to you. Remember how you were talking about needing someone with mad skills in content creation and killer marketing? Well, this person fits the bill perfectly!"

"She is a distant cousin of Kayla, and she could be the perfect fit for what you're looking for. I can reach out to her on short notice if needed," he added.

"Great! Set up a meeting ASAP, I am ready," I responded eagerly.

The COVID-19 pandemic undeniably introduced game-changing shifts in people's lives, reshaping many facets of our society. Our company encountered a notable post-COVID challenge in the demand sector, particularly in the field of marketing and sales. The pandemic's profound impact on public health and safety introduced a significant disruption in the equilibrium of these sectors.

One of the most prominent transformations in the post-COVID era was the shift in consumer perception and priorities, specifically concerning hygiene and safety.

The public's heightened awareness of health risks necessitated a fundamental change in how hotels and resorts approached marketing and sales. Gaining the confidence of the public in terms of hygiene and safety measures became paramount, and it substantially altered the dynamics of the industry.

In this new landscape, businesses had to adapt swiftly, implementing stringent health and safety protocols, and effectively communicating these measures to their potential customers.

Despite putting in extensive effort and implementing various measures, the hotel and resort segment of Wadia's has yet to experience a full recovery.

What's more, a recent digital advertising campaign deployed by a competitor has significantly impacted our share prices. This unexpected development has presented a notable challenge for our business.

Engrossed in managing all the details and handling files, I didn't notice the passing time until my phone interrupted the momentum with a ringing tone.

It was Kabir on the other end, "Hey, where are you, man?"

"I'm still at the office," I replied.

He sounded shocked, "What? Do you even know what time it is?"

"Umm... Yeah, I just lost track. I was absorbed in working on some data and figures," I tried to explain.

"Neil, it's 6 a.m.," Kabir responded in disbelief.

I was equally surprised by the revelation and sheepishly admitted, "Oh, I didn't realize."

"Okay, no worries. I'm on my way. Oh, and by the way, I managed to contact the marketing expert, and we are on the way," Kabir informed me.

"Great! See you then".

"Done," Kabir disconnected the call.

As I glanced at the clock, I was taken aback at how quickly time was passing. It was then that I took a good look around my newly revamped office for the first time.

Despite my numerous objections, Kabir had gone ahead with the refurbishment, convinced that a touch of luxury was essential.

He chuckled, "Oh Neil, my humble-hearted millionaire, why don't you let the team decide how your high-rise office should look?"

While I'm not particularly fond of extravagance, looking around my office at this moment, I appreciated the overall result of Kabir's vision.

The entire process of refurbishing had just been completed last week, and with the dawn of a new day creeping in, the sight gave me a sense of relief.

I found myself in awe of the sheer magnificence that surrounded me. The room was vast, adorned with towering ceilings that seemed to reach the heavens. Above, crystal chandeliers cast a soft, warm glow, illuminating the space and infusing it with an air of grandeur.

The furnishings exuded an undeniable sense of luxury and refinement. Every piece seemed carefully chosen to convey prestige and success, from the polished, custom-made desk at the center of the room to the plush leather chairs that beckoned with irresistible comfort.

The desk, an impressive masterpiece, boasted exquisite craftsmanship with its flawless blend of fine wood and sleek glass. Proudly displayed on the walls were pieces of art that spoke volumes about the impeccable taste and discerning eye. Framed degrees and awards spoke of my achievements earned through dedication and relentless pursuit of excellence. And through the floor-to-ceiling windows, the breathtaking city skyline teased onlookers, offering a mesmerizing view of success in its purest form.

Accents of elegance were scattered throughout the space. Fresh flowers in meticulously arranged vases filled the air with delicate scents. Sculptures, carefully selected and placed, added a touch of sophistication.

Meanwhile, richly designed rugs adorned the floor, their patterns reflecting the flawless attention to detail.

This office was a testament to power, prosperity, and the highest echelons of success. It was more than just a workspace; it was a sanctuary where ideas flourished and dreams became reality.

This was more than an office; it was a reflection of a life lived on the apex of luxury.

I rose from my chair, where I had been seated throughout the night. After refreshing myself and washing my face, I eagerly awaited the arrival of Kabir and the marketing expert, who were on their way.

"Hey Maa! I'm sorry for missing your calls. I was caught up in something unexpected. How are you? How is Jodhpur? Ummmm... I hope everything is fine... Please visit soon. Love you." I hastily sent the message after seeing a bunch of missed calls from Mom, and then I plopped back down in my seat.

I could hear footsteps approaching my location, so I quickly gathered up and organized the clutter on my desk.

A notification appeared on my screen as soon as I had a glass of water. It was an email from the board committee,

"Hey, Mr. Wadia, we highly appreciate the comprehensive plan you shared in your email on time. It sounds very promising and strategic. The share market is projected to recover soon. Thank you for your dedication and attention to detail."

I sighed in relief as the clouds began to dissipate, feeling a sense of achievement. I was eager to share the news with Kabir.

However, the matter was not entirely resolved. We needed to promptly respond with an excellent marketing strategy and provide detailed information. Investors can be quite challenging to comprehend once they start sensing negativity in the market.

The situation was extremely delicate, especially considering that we had recently secured substantial funding of millions of dollars just last month. Naturally, we wanted to avoid any turbulence in this area.

I was engrossed in my laptop when Kabir entered my office, accompanied by an elegant young lady carrying a laptop bag.

Kabir was excited, "Hey, good morning, buddy! Allow me to introduce you to the esteemed Ms. Tara Patel. I told her all about what we're dealing with, and trust me, she's exactly who we need."

"Tara is a true digital marketing maven, has a proven track record of propelling numerous corporations and industries to new heights through her innovative strategies. Her knack for crafting advertisements that resonate with the sentiments of the general public is nothing short of remarkable. These ads, once unleashed, ignite like wildfire and swiftly transform into digital sensations.

Tara's expertise and creative genius in the world of digital marketing have undoubtedly left an indelible mark on the industry, and her impact continues to reverberate across the digital landscape.

She's got this amazing knack for turning things around and has worked wonders for big-name brands worldwide. I gave her a shout last night, and she wasted no time and hopped on a plane. I picked her up from the airport. And now, here she is, ready to help you out."

"Hello, Ms. Patel! Good morning, and thanks a ton for making it here so quickly. I hope your flight went smoothly without any hassles. Please, have a seat," I said warmly.

"Hello, Mr. Wadia! Good morning to you, too. I just wanted to say how honored I am to have the chance to work with you. Mr. Ahuja told me everything I needed to know, and I've come up with many ideas and details we should discuss. I truly believe these fresh concepts will help strengthen your real estate segment, which has been facing some tough competition lately," She replied eloquently.

Midst my musings, her words interrupted my train of thought, "Also, congratulations, sir. As a young entrepreneur gracing the front pages of esteemed magazines, it is a monumental achievement deserving of commendation."

"Thank you sincerely; your kindness is truly appreciated," I responded gratefully.

Suddenly, Kabir intervened, "Bro, before we delve deeper into our tasks, let me arrange some coffee and breakfast. You've been toiling all night. Take a moment to relax, and then we can collaboratively work on the ideas proposed by Ms. Patel."

I countered, "I am alright. Let's formulate our strategy for the day first. It won't consume much time. Afterwards, we can enjoy breakfast together. I reckon Ms. Patel may also require sustenance."

"Ms. Patel, allow me to delve into the intricate details of your comprehensive plan for addressing the ongoing market crisis at Wadia's. With your permission, I would like to initiate the process of formulating the next steps to tackle this pressing issue ASAP." I added, addressing Ms. Patel.

Ms. Patel, well-prepared with the full presentation slides on the matter, promptly opened her laptop and commenced her explanation,

"People's perceptions and fears regarding COVID-19 have significantly impacted their preferences, particularly when it comes to avoiding hotels and resorts. This shift in consumer behavior stems from various concerns, such as health and safety. We need to understand these concerns and strategically tailor our approach to reassure potential guests and adapt to the new landscape."

"In this new equillibrium, businesses have to adapt swiftly, implementing stringent health and safety protocols, and effectively communicating these measures to their potential customers. Trust and reassurance regarding a clean and secure environment will become essential selling points. Marketing strategies need to emphasize these aspects, and sales efforts have to align with the changing consumer preferences. Ultimately, this challenge will serve as a catalyst for innovation and creativity in the marketing and sales sectors, as companies strive to regain the trust and confidence of the public in a post-COVID world.

"If you've observed, Mr. Wadia, our competitor 'Roy Estates' has recently launched a campaign that effectively caters to and addresses these critical concerns. They've made a strong emotional connection with the public. We now have the opportunity to step up our game and surpass their efforts."

"Do you have something specific in mind, Ms. Patel?" I got curious.

She continued,

"Creating a digital campaign that can rebuild public trust in the post-COVID era requires a thoughtful approach. Here's a strategic outline for such a campaign:

Campaign Title:

'SafeStay: Your Well-Being, Our Priority'

"The goal is to create a digital campaign that not only reassures the public but also positions our hotels and resorts as leaders in ensuring safety and well-being during these challenging times."

She continued her explanation without pause, her words flowing seamlessly as she delved deeper into the intricacies of the campaign strategy..

After investing nearly two hours, we completed our tasks. Ms Patel's expertise was evident; she possessed a clear understanding of what needed to be done. With our day schedule meticulously prepared, we set off for a well-deserved breakfast.

Kabir voiced his concern, "Bro, you must get some serious rest now. I'll call Ashok, and he will arrange for your transportation home. Tara and I will manage the rest."

Ms. Patel chimed in, "Indeed, sir, "Please have some rest."

We agreed to reconvene later to discuss the report.

Subsequently, the rest of the team delved into their respective tasks while I departed with Ashok, hoping to catch some much-needed rest at home.

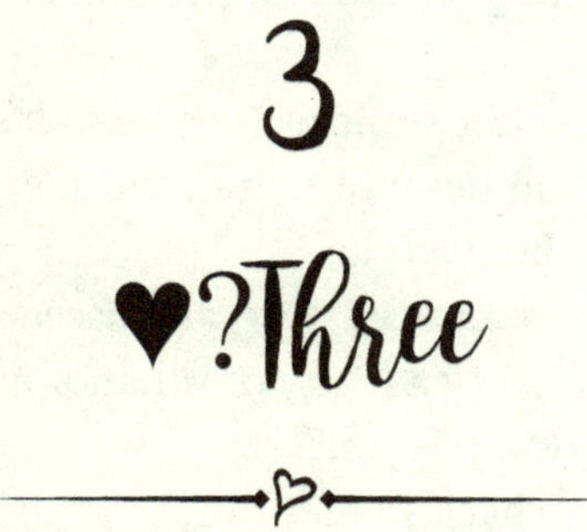

3

♥?Three

I was abruptly awakened by the persistent ringing of my phone. It turned out to be Kabir.

With an enthusiastic tone, he exclaimed, "Bro, things are great again! Our digital campaign has taken off amazingly, and it's going viral now."

"At that very moment, the office felt incomplete without you. Let's meet up in about an hour. We're having a small gathering at my place. See you then."

"Hey, Sounds great; congratulations to you, too. Ms Patel has done some wonders. Will meet you there," I responded, hanging up the phone.

Desiring a few more moments of slumber, I attempted to fall back asleep. However, the phone persisted in ringing. Every investor, board member, and the rest of the world seemed to be trying to reach me.

Amidst the commotion, an email from Ms. Patel caught my attention, "Congratulations, sir. Everything is back on track."

I couldn't help but smile as I replied, "It's all because of you, Ms. Patel. You deserve more than mere appreciation. Let's meet up in the evening."

Subsequently, I noticed several missed calls from my mom, accompanied by a flurry of WhatsApp messages:

"Hello, Beta. How are you?"

"Please call me back soon."

"Mrs. Reddy has sent over some profiles of girls for you to consider. Take a look, they are nice. I want you to find a suitable partner and settle down soon."

My mother has been persistently urging me to get married for the past few years, and it seems like a common desire among Indian mothers.

However, I've never felt that urge or charm to settle down with someone unknown and unfamiliar. Falling in love was something that seemed out of the question for me, given my straightforward nature and introverted personality.

You can only imagine the number of wedding proposals and romantic pursuits I've turned down by the time I reached my early thirties. Last month, when Kabir got engaged to Kayla, my mom seemed more saddened by the fact that I was the only one left without a partner.

I suppose Kabir has become my designated wingman in my mother's quest to find a suitable match for me.

At the moment, I knew exactly how to respond to those proposals sent by Mrs. Reddy. I don't even bother looking at the profiles she sends me because the idea of arranged marriage simply doesn't resonate with me.

Some had been drawn to wealth, others to fame, and there had even been some who were enchanted by my mother's kind heart and incredible nature.

Now, I've come to accept the notion that there is no harm in living a life without a partner.

Back in college, I was the matchmaker responsible for bringing Kabir and Kayla together. But, truth be told, I wasn't really on the lookout for someone for myself. Even though there were plenty of intelligent and successful girls around, it just never crossed my mind to give it a shot.

My primary and ultimate goal in life was to make my dad proud, and in pursuit of that, I might have missed out on some beautiful ways to live life to the fullest.

My love for my dad is immeasurable. He holds a special place in my heart that no one else could fill. From the moment I was born, he was my protector, guide, and hero.

He was always there for me, providing unwavering support and encouragement.

His unconditional love was truly remarkable. I could always count on him to lend a listening ear, offer wise advice, or simply be a comforting presence. His words of wisdom resonate deeply within me and shape the person I am becoming.

My dad's selflessness inspires me every day—his dedication to our well-being and happiness.

The bond I shared with my dad is profound. We have shared countless laughs, tears, and unforgettable memories. Whether watching movies together, going on adventures, or simply spending quality time, every moment with him was precious and cherished.

I am grateful for every lesson he has taught me, every hug he has given, and every smile he has brought to my face, and I am forever thankful to have him as my father.

When I graduated at the top of my class at Stanford, my dad was genuinely proud and thrilled. My mom was over the moon with happiness.

Two years later, a wave of unbearable sorrow washed over our lives as we bid farewell to Dad. The pain of losing him shattered our hearts into a million pieces, leaving us feeling lost and devastated. To find solace, I plunged myself into work, immersing in the vision and legacy Dad had built.

It became my refuge, the only place I could channel my thoughts and pour my energy as I yearned for a sense of purpose and connection to our precious memories.

The absence of Dad weighed heavily on Mom's heart, to the point that it took a toll on her health. The depth of her longing for him was so profound that she fell ill all too often.

Unfortunately, my preoccupation with work only added to her burden. After a year of witnessing her suffering, she decided to move to her sister's home in Jodhpur. It was a bittersweet choice, as it meant she could find solace in the company of loved ones and have someone to share her life with. It was a small consolation amidst the overwhelming grief that consumed us all.

Regardless, my mom will not give up on the pursuit of finding my match, and I will simply have to learn to live with the constant stream of messages from Mrs. Reddy.

Engulfed by a storm of incessant thoughts and overwhelming emotions, I struggled to find the strength to face the day. The weight of the world seemed to press down upon my shoulders, making even the simplest tasks feel insurmountable.

After what felt like an eternity, I slowly mustered the courage to rise from the comfort of my bed.

The sun had long passed its zenith, casting long shadows throughout the room. It was already 4 p.m., and a sense of guilt washed over me for allowing the hours to slip away unnoticed.

I shuffled towards the bathroom, my footsteps heavy and lethargic. The sound of water cascading from the showerhead filled the air, offering a momentary reprieve from the chaos within my mind. The cool droplets splashed against my skin, awakening my senses and ushering in a faint glimmer of clarity.

I tried to steel myself against the onslaught of memories and flashbacks of happier times, but the images persisted, like fragments of shattered glass embedded deep within my consciousness.

Finally, with a heavy sigh and a deep breath of resolve, I emerged from the bathroom. I stood in front of the mirror, gazing into my weary eyes, seeking a glimmer of strength to carry me through the day.

Kabir's place beckoned, offering a temporary respite from the solace of my thoughts. I hoped that amidst his company, amidst the familiarity of shared experiences and shared laughter, I could find fleeting moments of respite from the whirlwind of emotions that threatened to pull me under.

As I approached Kabir's abode, a sense of anticipation washed over me. Kabir's place, known for its radiant energy and welcoming ambiance, was brimming with people. The air hummed with the mingling of voices, filling the grand living hall with a sense of life and vitality.

The walls, adorned with art and photographs captured in moments of pure bliss, radiated with the echoes of joy and camaraderie. The decor itself told stories of laughter, tears, and all the shades of emotions that make up the tapestry of life.

The living hall, with its high ceilings and expansive windows, felt like an oasis of rejuvenation amid a chaotic world. Sunbeams streamed in, casting a warm glow upon everyone gathered, illuminating their physical presence and the internal light that danced within.

The room buzzed with conversation, the symphony of voices interweaving, creating a harmonious melody. Laughter erupted like a chorus, cascading through the air and infusing the space with an infectious joy. The fragrance of delectable food wafted through the room, tantalizing the senses and awakening the appetite for culinary delights and connection.

Amidst the bustling crowd, faces old and new, I felt a sense of belonging, a brief respite from the weight of my grief. The collective energy and the shared experiences breathed life into the once-empty corners of my soul.

I found solace in the ebb and flow of conversations, the gentle touch of shoulders brushing against mine, and the exchange of knowing glances that spoke volumes without uttering a word.

In that grand living hall, I felt a renewed sense of hope. It was a reminder that life, though often marred by sorrow and loss, possessed an incredible capacity for growth and renewal.

Kabir has always been fond of throwing parties, and he thoroughly enjoys playing the role of the host. He knows I tend to arrive late and leave early, but he still manages to engage with me.

Finally, he is taking the plunge, sealing his bond with the love of his life, Kayla. Their union is not merely the coming together of two individuals but a testament to the enduring power of love and the promise of a lifetime of togetherness.

Back in our college days, I used to organize special dates and thoughtful events in the hopes of bringing them together.

Kayla was always astounded by my ability to perceive the subtlest expressions of love between her and Kabir, even when they remained blissfully unaware.

It was as if I possessed an innate gift, a sixth sense that allowed me to witness their profound connection, even when it lay hidden beneath their conscious awareness.

The day Kabir finally mustered the courage to propose to her, a twinkle of excitement danced in her eyes as she beckoned me closer. With a heartfelt embrace, Kayla whispered, "You are the brother I never had.".

She was always brilliant, and Kabir is the epitome of fun. Seeing them together, it's evident that they are truly meant for each other.

As expected, there are several colleagues from the office, some old friends, and even Kayla, accompanied by her friends, who have been suggested as potential romantic interests for me. After a few interactions, they have probably realized that I am not the most exciting person to be around.

However, Kayla holds a different opinion. According to her, I am one of the world's most romantic and sensible men, second only to Kabir (of course). As I stood there, watching them together, I couldn't help but feel a surge of pride for Kabir's courage and the love that had woven its way into their lives.

It was an honor to have played a small part in their journey, witnessed their love story unfold, and been trusted with their deepest emotions.

My chain of thoughts always seems to go on indefinitely, but this time, it was interrupted by Kayla. As soon as she saw me at the entrance of the hall, she rushed over and gave me a warm hug, exclaiming,

"Come on, you're the man of today's show, dude! Come, come!"

Kabir, who hails from a business family with multiple segments overseen by his father and brother, followed closely behind Kayla. His joyous reaction to seeing me was to give me a tight hug.

Upon entering, Kabir showed me the video campaign that Ms. Patel had launched. To my astonishment, it had already garnered a significant number of views in just three hours.

Undeniably, her talent is unparalleled. Although our company boasts several marketing experts and campaign specialists, none of them could have captured the emotions of the common man as she did.

As I ventured further into the hall, attention was drawn to Ms. Patel standing alone, engrossed in her phone as if she was monitoring the progress of the incredible work she had accomplished.

"Hey, Ms. Patel! Congratulations on your incredible work and the success of the ad. Everyone is buzzing about it. You have truly made an impact in our lives, madam," I approached her and expressed my admiration.

"Oh, Hello, sir!" she exclaimed, her voice brimming with excitement and gratitude. Every word she spoke carried a genuine appreciation for the chance bestowed upon her.

"Thank you so much for giving me this incredible opportunity. Working with you has been an absolute joy, a truly enriching experience that I will treasure always."

Tara's gratitude and admiration for me and my team radiated through her voice, her words carrying a genuine heartfelt appreciation. It was a testament to the positive work environment I had fostered—a place where people were inspired to give their best, collaborating harmoniously to achieve extraordinary results.

"I am delighted to have you gracing our presence, Ms. Patel. Extensive gratitude is owed to Kabir for unveiling such a concealed gem to our discerning eyes," I exclaimed, expressing my sincere appreciation for her presence.

"Thank you sir", She replied politely

"Also, May I make a request, Please?" She added.

"Yes, Please!", I replied with grace and encouragement.

"Please address me as Tara, as that name holds a deep significance for me, sir," Ms. Patel requested politely.

"Sure, but on one condition," I smiled warmly.

"And what might that be?" She was taken aback by my proposal.

"Well, I have learned that you plan to leave for Mumbai tomorrow. I would like to offer you a permanent position as the Marketing Head in our prestigious FMCG segment at Wadia Industries. It would be incredibly fortunate for us to have you in Gurgaon," I earnestly offered.

Her surprise was evident in her body language as my words sunk in. She delicately touched her forehead and smiled, brimming with astonishment.

"Are you certain about this? It would be a great honor to collaborate with you, sir. Although I have never intended to work with corporations, I like it here." she replied, her voice filled with gratitude.

"I want to assure you, Tara, that this is the greatest opportunity we can ever have. Do I have your permission to discuss the matter with Kabir? I hope he shares our confidence," I declared with conviction.

"I'm afraid, sir, that I have some doubts," Tara expressed with a hint of sadness. She knew the dynamics of Kabir's relationships and how he preferred to keep his professional and family life separate. "Being distantly related to Kayla, Kabir approached me for this assignment out of genuine concern for your well-being. I responded swiftly to his call and came here. However, I fear that he may not agree to a permanent part, as he is firm in his resolve. Furthermore, I would never want to disappoint him, as our bond is profound," Tara explained honestly.

"What? Why was I not aware of this?" I exclaimed in shock.

Just then, Kayla approached us, brimming with excitement. "Ah, my two favorite people brought together at this moment. How fortunate!" she exclaimed.

"Kayla, I am truly astonished by this revelation that you know Tara and that both you and Kabir have kept such incredible talent hidden from Wadia Industries. Our company has been longing for marketing heads of her caliber," I exclaimed, my voice reflecting a mix of surprise and disbelief.

"Yes, Kabir has a policy of excluding relatives from his professional endeavors. While he occasionally seeks assistance from Tara, it is never permanent," Kayla smiled.

"This situation is absurd! I will talk to Kabir," I passionately added.

"Do you know, Neil, that Kayla is a talented wordsmith? She has written many fictional works and organizes captivating poetry showcases. Her creative skills in content writing are so remarkable that she works as a virtuoso freelancer."

"It is a mystery why she has turned down offers from prestigious companies, choosing instead to dedicate her time to literature and art," Kayla revealed.

Tara's smile filled the room, as she gazed at Kayla with affection in her eyes.

"Wonderful! Tara," I exclaimed, "Regardless, if you agree, you can join us for a short-term project, lasting at least a year.

As for Kabir, I will personally deal with any reservations he may have," I assured her.

"Tara, consider yourself fortunate that Neil appreciates your qualities. Otherwise, he has a peculiar talent for making people feel invisible," Kayla quipped, her laughter filling the room.

Tara, slightly uncomfortable by Kayla's playful remark, mustered a smile and replied, "Indeed, Mr. Wadia, I would be pleased to work with Wadia Industries, albeit for a limited time. I am genuinely impressed by the values upheld by your organization."

A few minutes later, She stepped out to receive a call.

After a while, Kabir approached me, "Hey, bro, care to have something? Perhaps a beer? Come on, loosen up."

"Hey, I'm just not in the mood right now, buddy," I looked at him with a smile.

"You always say that at every party. Today, no excuses," he insisted, and promptly ordered a drink for me.

As I soaked in the feeling of accomplishment, I decided to step outside into the open area of the hall and enjoy some fresh air. Tara was already there, checking her phone. We made eye contact, smiled at each other, and tried to enjoy the chilly breeze of October.

Feeling hospitable, I asked, "Hey, would you like anything to drink?"

"Thank you for offering, sir, but I don't drink alcohol," she smiled softly.

"Ah, my apologies. In that case, may I offer you a soft drink?" I insisted.

"Nah, I've already had a few. I'm good, sir," she again smiled gently.

She couldn't resist constantly checking her phone in between.

Keeping the conversation light, I flashed a smile, "So, do you always work at parties?"

"No, no," she replied warmly, "It's just a matter of keeping track of the figures. Nothing more."

I looked at Tara, "So, you're staying then?"

"Frankly, I haven't decided yet, but yes, I am considering the option, sir," She looked back at me.

"Okay, in that case, you have to report to the office sharp at 10:00 a.m. tomorrow," I added with a smile.

Tara responded with a soft smile. Just then, Kabir approached us, "How are you guys holding up? The actual party is inside if you want to join." He chuckled softly.

"Kabir, I have some news to share with you," I tapped his shoulder.

"Please, shoot, brother."

"First thing in the morning, you have to hire Tara as our marketing head of the FMCG segment," I declared.

"What? But..." Kabir muttered, taken aback by my statement.

"Kabir, no ifs, no buts," I insisted. "We want her in the team, and you know that."

"I'm okay if you want to keep her, but Tara doesn't work with corporates," Kabir expressed his concern.

"I have insisted, and she has agreed. So, she is joining us tomorrow," I reaffirmed my decision.

"Okay boss, always at your service," Kabir smiled, giving me a friendly tap on the back.

"Alright guys, I have to go and report to my girl, Kayla now, so please excuse me," He chuckled softly and went inside.

We shared a smile as Kabir walked away, leaving just the two of us to continue our conversation.

"So, Finally, Welcome to the team, Tara," I added softly.

"Sir, thank you so very much. It is an honor to work with you," Tara smiled gratefully.

"Okay, one more thing. Since you are officially a part of the team, no need for 'sir' anymore. It makes me feel like a 50-year-old man with a bald head. Just call me Neil, please. That's what everybody says," I replied, trying to lighten the mood.

With a graceful smile, she nodded in agreement.

I wished Tara a good night and said my farewells to Kabir and Kayla before heading towards my home. Kabir, knowing that I wouldn't be staying much longer, responded with a good night as well.

It has been a few days since Tara joined the office, and she has proven to be exceptionally good at her work. Our digital and offline marketing efforts have been incredibly successful, surpassing our competitors. We are riding a new wave of success.

Since the party at Kabir's, I haven't had a chance to catch up with her. Everyone seems to be busy with their tasks. Kayla, in particular, is swamped with preparations for her upcoming wedding.

My mom still hasn't come to terms with my decision not to get married. Mrs. Reddy continues to send marriage proposals almost daily, but I delete them without even looking.

Ana is always occupied with her desk duties and making sure I have my daily dose of green tea.

As for me, I am fully engrossed in my work in the luxurious office. Sometimes, I miss my old office, which had a nostalgic feel with my late father's belongings. Perhaps, Kabir changed everything to avoid dwelling on our loss.

It's like trying to decipher the Bermuda Triangle of his mind—I'm perpetually clueless about what's happening in there!

This time, my chain of thoughts was interrupted by Kabir entering the office, "Hey dude, let's catch up tonight at my place. It's Kayla's birthday, nothing fancy, just close friends." Kabir seemed eager and excited.

"Oh man, I completely forgot. Let me call her up," I felt guilty.

"No, don't call her. Just come to the party and surprise her. She'll be so happy. And by the way, could you pick up the cake? I'll text you the address," Kabir responded.

"Sure, I'll be there. Just Whatsapp me the timings.", I nodded,

Kabir was in a hurry, so he left without saying much. It was understandable - he had to throw the best party of the century tonight.

I quickly got back to work and started wrapping things up as I had to rush to the party and pick up the cake along the way. The evening roads can get jammed with traffic in Gurgaon, and I wanted to avoid the couple's complaints.

I arrived at Kabir's place on time, holding the cake in my hands. As soon as I entered, I made my way towards Kayla and wished her a happy birthday. Her face lit up with pure joy upon seeing me.

The party was a grand celebration organized by Kabir. As soon as guests stepped into the venue, they were greeted by an atmosphere of joy and excitement. The decorations were opulent, with elegant floral arrangements and sparkling lights adorning the entire space.

Kabir had spared no expense in creating a lavish setting for the occasion, leaving everyone impressed. Kayla, dressed in stunning attire befitting the special day, exuded elegance and radiance. She wore a beautiful gown that complemented her features perfectly, capturing the attention of all those present. Kabir couldn't take his eyes off her, and their happiness was evident in their smiles and laughter throughout the evening.

It was a perfect blend of entertainment and heartfelt moments. There was a live band playing uplifting music, encouraging guests to hit the dance floor and let loose.

Delicious food and drinks were served, with a carefully curated menu that catered to every palate. From mouth-watering appetizers to decadent desserts, every culinary detail had been carefully considered. The couple's love for exquisite cuisine was evident in the selection and presentation of the dishes.

The night was filled with warmth, laughter, and beautiful memories. Friends and family shared heartfelt toasts and wished Kayla a happy birthday. The atmosphere was charged with love and affection, as everyone celebrated the joyous occasion alongside the couple.

Overall, the party was a testament to their happiness and commitment to celebrating life's special moments in style. It was a night to remember, filled with love, laughter, and an abundance of bliss.

Amidst the bustling party atmosphere, my gaze landed on Tara.

From what I've observed, Tara seemed to possess this inherent quality of authenticity. She never felt the need to mold herself into someone else's version or blend in with the prevailing atmosphere. Instead, she preserved her own distinct space, radiating a contagious positivity and refreshing energy that had a remarkable impact on those fortunate enough to be in her presence.

Following the enchanting cake ceremony, I ventured out to the spacious lawn, seeking solace with a refreshing beer in hand.

To my delightful surprise, there she was - Tara, already settled on a stool, cradling a cup of chilled coffee with utmost care in her hands.

"Hi there, didn't expect to see you here," Tara greeted with a smile.

"Hey, yeah. Kabir loves throwing parties, and somehow, he always ends up inviting me," I returned the smile.

"They are truly a perfect match, Kabir and Kayla," She chuckled softly.

"Yes. Indeed," I looked upon her.

Curiosity bubbling inside me like a fizzy soda, I couldn't help but blurt out, "So, what's new with you? How do you like your new job and office?"

With contagious enthusiasm, She responded, "Oh, let me tell you, I'm digging it here! The vibes are so positive, and the place is teeming with vibrant souls who just light up the atmosphere."

Amidst a chuckle, I couldn't resist, "So, I'm guessing you have a strict no-alcohol policy here too, huh?"

"Oh, yes. And honestly, I must admit, this coffee feels a bit stronger than I expected," Tara smiled back.

"Lol," I was amused by her response.

"So, why aren't you inside with the rest of the friends?" I was curious.

"I'm still getting acquainted with the group, and I must admit, I have quite reservations when it comes to choosing friends," she explained with a hint of caution in her voice.

I flashed a smile, "Ah, got it!"

Meanwhile, we conversed lightly, the background was filled with a mix of lively chatter, laughter, and the pleasant hum of music. People mingled, exchanging stories and catching up with old friends. Some participants were engrossed in animated discussions, while others took advantage of the moment to grab a drink or find a comfortable spot to relax. The atmosphere was vibrant, creating a vibrant ambiance.

To make Tara feel at ease, I asked casually, "So, Tell me about your interests. Are you a foodie, someone who enjoys parties, or perhaps there's something else that used to keep you engaged back in Mumbai?"

Deep in thought, she smiled, "Hmm... I would say I'm quite spontaneous. One day, I might enjoy a trip to the movies, while on another, delight in indulging in panipuri. There are times when I find solace in going alone to coffee shops or quiet spots to write."

"And now and then, I simply love the process of canvassing, although it's a bit of a struggle here since all my setups are back in Mumbai."

"I must say, you're quite an intriguing girl, Tara," I remarked. "I can't fathom going somewhere alone and having a meal by myself. Even though I often have my meals alone, be it at the office or home, the thought of going out solo to eat just feels peculiar to me."

"I completely understand," She empathized.

"It can feel complex and unfamiliar. However, you're always welcome to join me the next time I go out to fill my taste buds." She chuckled softly

"Sounds like a plan. Count me in!" I seemed excited. "Just give me a heads up."

As I continued conversing with her, a thought lingered in my mind. I couldn't help but ponder why and how I found this interaction with her so captivating.

Typically, I would dismiss such conversations as a waste of time or meaningless, but with her, there was a distinct shift. She possessed a magnetic aura that drew people in, and I found myself genuinely relishing her company.

"I heard about your dad. I'm sorry for your loss, Neil," Her eyes flashed with sympathy.

"Thank you," I responded warmly.

"I still feel his absence deeply. Sometimes, it feels like he's still around. In moments when I feel lost, I watch his old videos where he delivered inspiring TED talks and lectures. It feels that he is talking to me through those words. But since his passing, work has kept me occupied.

She displayed a compassionate smile and gracefully took a sip of her coffee.

I couldn't help but notice a magnetic pull towards her, feeling a sense of lightheadedness whenever she was near.

Her friendly and joyful nature made her a delightful presence to be around. However, amidst her smile, I sensed that hidden emotions were being concealed with perfection.

I shrugged off my shoulders and allowed myself to get lost in my thoughts. The evening was pleasant, with a cool breeze gently blowing. The company was perfect, the drink was perfect. It was everything I could have ever wished for.

We continued talking and lost track of time. It was a surprise to both of us when we finally noticed the dawn approaching. We glanced at our watches and couldn't believe it was already 5 a.m.

Chuckling and shocked at the same time, we decided it was time to leave. Stepping back into the hall, we noticed a few people still chatting and drinking, but most had already left or fallen asleep.

We tried to find Kabir and Kayla, but they were nowhere to be found. I left a message for Kabir, "Hey buddy, we're leaving. See you at the office."

Ashok was already waiting outside for me. The day was just beginning, with the first rays of sunlight appearing on the horizon.

A week passed by, and Monday arrived with a packed schedule of meetings and tasks. The day was already planned out by Ana.

It was already noon, I hadn't even had my morning green tea, and my gym session had been particularly tiring.

Glancing at my phone, I scrolled through messages and attempted to reply to Mom's calls when suddenly Tara's message popped up,

"Hey, what's up... Heading out for some pani puris. You wanna join?"

"If yes, meet me near the big mango tree beside the valet parking."

A smile adorned my face as I contemplated, "She is truly the embodiment of vibrancy on this earth."

I started typing a response, intending to decline and continue with my busy day. But something changed at that moment. Before I knew it, I was calling Ana to cancel my meetings for the next two hours.

Finally, I typed, "On my way," and stepped outside my office. Honestly, the idea of stepping out to enjoy pani puris seemed unusual to me, but I walked out nonetheless.

As I reached my parking spot, I found Ashok waiting inside the car. Starting the car, I parked myself under the shade of the mango tree, waiting for Tara. After about five minutes, she arrived and we set off to satisfy her craving for pani puris.

While giving me a map to follow, She smiled,

"I didn't expect that you would come."

"Me neither," I smiled back.

Tara's voice filled the air as she constantly shared stories and thoughts, and I found myself completely enthralled by her company. She possessed a magnetic combination of wit and energy that made conversing with her a delight.

I was enjoying her chatty nature. It felt like a different version of myself, the sadness and unattended emotions started to disperse off just being in her company.

Curiosity sparked within me as I opened up, "Tell me something about your college, I imagine it must have been fun."

A hint of shyness appeared in her eyes as she chuckled softly,

"Ohh no... no, Neil. You won't believe it, I was incredibly shy during my college time. My friends used to tease me forever."

"What? I can't believe that," I exclaimed, realizing I may have revealed too much enthusiasm.

“A lot has changed in the past few years,” she said. “I am a different person now.” She smiled and looked at me.

I was surprised by her words but contained my Curiosity.

"You won't believe once back in college, I dared to propose to a random guy in the cafeteria. I got down on one knee, but that poor boy was so frightened that he ran away like anything. The entire cafeteria witnessed the moment, and everyone began calling me the 'Proposal girl since then.' I had to live with that name forever." Her excitement was visible in her tone.

"That day, I made two promises...

1. I would never play dare again, and

2. I would never propose to anyone in my life."

She continued chuckling softly.

"That must have been humiliating for some guys," I smiled, amused by the image.

"Hahahaha...Guys aren't interested in me anyway. According to many of my friends, I'm a total bore, especially at parties."

I stayed silent, yearning to express how special she truly was, but the words eluded me at that moment.

As we arrived at our location, Tara ordered the 'pani puris', and we began to savor them.

With my first bite, the spiciness exploded, causing me to burst out with a mixture of surprise and heat. Tara couldn't help but laugh.

"Neil, I guess you're not fond of 'pani puris'."

"But you know what's fun about eating them?"

Tara's laughter danced in the air

"They're so spicy when you eat them, they manage to make you forget all the stress in the moment and clear your mind."

I looked at her recovering from the spice-induced shock,

"Tara, your perspective on the world is completely different."

"Alright then, Get me bombarded with more 'pani puris'", I laughed, eagerly reaching for another one.

"I want to make sure my head is crystal clear right away."

And so, we continued to indulge in the moment, sharing laughter, stories, and an unspoken connection that grew stronger with each passing second.

As I was about to park the car, my phone rang. It was Kabir calling to tell me that he was at the office and wanted to discuss something with both me and Tara.

"I'm on my way, she's with me. We'll be there soon," I replied, sharing the news with Tara.

We walked towards my office, anticipation filling the air.

As we entered, Kabir eagerly awaited us, bursting with excitement. "Bro, the date is finalized... the marriage is in two months. Finally, I and Kayla are going to be together. We are having a destination wedding in Goa," he exclaimed.

Overwhelmed with happiness, I embraced Kabir, knowing that this would be the most significant day of his life.

Emotion welled up in his eyes, and Tara joined me in congratulating him. The atmosphere shimmered with joy and celebration.

"By the way, where were you guys off to?" Kabir anxiously looked upon us."

"Tara invited me to have some pani puris, so we went out," I looked back at Kabir gently.

"Guys, I'm a lone eater too. Please count me on these small dates," Kabir insisted.

Tara looked upon us with a spark in her eyes.

"Hey, why don't we have lunch together like whenever our schedules match? That way, no one will eat alone."

"Excellent idea. See you both tomorrow for lunch in Neil's office," Kabir almost jumped with excitement before leaving to answer a call.

Tara stood by the large window, gazing out at the view.

"You know, I like this mango tree near the entrance. It exudes a sense of wisdom and age." She was deep in her thoughts.

"This tree holds a special place in my heart. My dad planted it 20 years ago when I was just a kid. Now, whenever I look at it, I feel as though he's watching over me through its branches," my words filled with sentiment.

Tara smiled softly and looked at me. " I know You miss him a lot, Neil. You were lucky to have him as your Dad." Her eyes were filled with a little sadness as she finished her words.

I nodded, gesturing for her to take a seat. However, she looked at her phone,

"Hey, I need to catch up with the team on the new Ad. I gotta go. Let's meet for lunch tomorrow. See you then."

Her words held a promise of future moments together, and with that, she left, leaving me longing for our next meeting.

The next morning arrived, busier than ever. The day was filled with non-stop calls and meetings, leaving me little time to breathe. Ana had kindly brought me three cups of green tea since morning, but they had all been forgotten and left to grow cold.

If it weren't for the vegetable juices prepared by my butler at home, I would have been severely dehydrated by now. Thankfully, the heavy breakfast has sustained me this far.

Amid my busy schedule, Kunwarji, our cook and a treasured presence in our office, knocked on my door. "Sir, your lunch is ready. May I bring it to you now?"

Kunwarji had been part of our family and the office since my father's time. When I was a child, he would often take me for walks around the campus, showing me the hidden corners and sharing stories.

Glancing at the clock, I realized that I was indeed hungry. Just as I was about to respond to Kunwarji, Kabir burst into the office with enthusiasm. "Hey bro, finish up quickly. It's lunchtime!"

I nodded to Kunwarji, acknowledging his offer, and stood up from my desk, ready to indulge in a much-needed meal.

While Kabir and I waited for Tara to join us, we discussed a few details from the previous day's meeting.

After approximately five minutes, She gracefully entered my office, carrying her lunch bag. She greeted us with excitement,

"Hey guys, sorry I'm a bit late. Give me a moment, then let's dive in. I'm seriously hungry."

Kunwarji had arrived with our meals, presenting the platter to Kabir and me. However, Tara politely declined, revealing that she had already brought her lunch.

As we began to eat, a sense of joy and connection filled the room. We talked, we laughed, and amidst it all, I couldn't help but notice a certain enchantment whenever Tara was around. Something about her presence had ignited a spark within me, and I couldn't deny the growing affection I felt.

Tara had chosen to bring rajma, Kabir's all-time favorite.

He playfully snatched her lunch from her, exclaiming, "This is mine... who cooked it, yaar? Please send your cook to our place sometimes. He is amazing."

Tara burst into laughter, "Sorry, Kabir, not possible. I cooked it myself. Cooking is my stress buster."

Kabir's laughter filled the room, his joy was contagious.

"Tara, trust me, if I weren't about to marry Kayla, I would have proposed to you right here."

Amidst the hilarity, Tara chuckled and quipped, "Just because of Rajma? I think you should have a few more reasons to marry someone than just their cooking."

Our laughter intermingled, creating a beautiful melody of shared moments and the promise of a deepening bond.

Days turned into weeks, and our lunches together in my office became a cherished routine. Occasionally, in the evenings, we would venture out for a leisurely stroll, indulging in delectable snacks or sharing a cup of coffee.

The three of us formed an unbreakable bond, growing closer with each passing moment. Sometimes, Kayla would join us, adding her vibrant energy to our gatherings. It was during these moments that I realized how much more alive my life had become since the day I met Tara.

Each interaction with her brought an undeniable spark, filling my days with joy and significance. Time seemed to fly in her presence, and every shared meal or laughter only deepened our connection. Something new was blossoming in the simplest moments, and I couldn't wait to see where this journey would lead us.

The delectable flavors of Tara's culinary creations had captured Kayla's heart. One fine day, unable to contain her excitement, Kayla cried out, her voice filled with longing,

"Tara, please invite us to your place for a casual dinner, yar. Let us eat till we burst into your kitchen."

Tara, beamed with joy, her voice carrying a melody of anticipation, "Absolutely, guys. Anytime would be perfect. Let us plan for the weekend ahead, coming Friday. What's say?"

In unison, Kabir and I nodded, our eyes sparkling with anticipation.

"Consider it done then," Tara chuckled merrily, her laughter floating through the air like music. "We shall meet on Friday evening at my place."

Kayla, her playful spirit shining through, chimed in with a mischievous chuckle,

"And fear not, Tara, we are gonna help you at least with chopping and basic preparations. What say you, boys?"

Kabir's eyes sparkled with eagerness, "Indeed, Darling. Whatever we can do to help Tara, we shall arrive early to help her out."

The once-muted office now thrived with newfound liveliness. The air was filled with an electrifying vibe, while the aura around us changed dramatically, radiating a sense of renewed energy and enchantment.

Friday had arrived, the eagerly anticipated day when we would all gather at Tara's home.

Typically, we would have our daily lunches as a group, but due to a particularly busy day, we had forgotten our usual meal.

With the day winding down, I decided to leave the office around 5, ensuring I had enough time to reach Tara's place for the planned dinner.

Oddly enough, I felt an extra burst of excitement for this dinner. It was unlike the usual office parties I attended, so I decided to break away from my customary office attire and instead opted for something more casual- a flurry of excitement danced within me.

I stood in front of my wardrobe, contemplating what to wear to capture the essence of this special moment. After a few minutes, I reached for a sleek black t-shirt, its dark hue promising an air of mystery. Pairing it with my favorite denim jeans, their indigo fabric exuding casual elegance, I felt a surge of confidence wash over me.

Stepping into my casual footwear, I embraced comfort without compromising on style. Their relaxed design perfectly complemented my chosen ensemble, striking a harmonious balance between ease and refinement.

With our plans in motion, I followed the location details that Tara had shared with us. The drive took approximately 40 minutes, but every mile covered was filled with excitement and energy.

Arriving at Tara's residence, I parked the car and walked up to her front door. With a sense of eagerness, I pressed the doorbell.

In just around 50 seconds, which felt like an eternity in my enthusiasm, the gate opened before me, revealing Tara's smiling face and a joyous sense of hope filled the air. Her long, luscious hair cascaded down her back in a messy braided style, adding an enchanting touch to her appearance. With every movement, her hair swayed like a gentle dance, embodying the sense of effortless beauty that radiated from within.

Her attire was a vibrant blue dress that hugged her silhouette, reaching just below her knees. The sparkling hue complemented her complexion and added a touch of elegance to her presence.

Tara greeted me with a warm welcome, as I handed her the bouquet of yellow roses that I had bought. The choice of flowers seemed fitting for the hour and occasion, and Tara's appreciation was evident in her grateful response.

"Thank you so much, Neil. These are so pretty," her words were brimming with sincerity. She invited me inside, gesturing towards the cozy sofa in her impeccably arranged living room.

Taking a moment to look around, I noticed how the house exuded an air of beauty, order, and affection. It felt like stepping into a haven of warmth and purity. Settling comfortably on the sofa, Tara apologized for being a bit late in finishing the preparations.

"No need to apologize," I reassured her with a smile.

"We're here to help you in the kitchen, remember?"

"Let's move there and work together. I may not be very skilled, but I can certainly assist with chopping and setting the table. I'm quite good at that."

Before Tara could respond, her phone began to ring. It was a call from Kayla, informing her that they were running late, and promised to make it up to her within the hour.

Tara welcomed me into her kitchen with a coy shrug of her shoulders. The sight before me was a testament to her dedication to creating a culinary masterpiece. The countertops were adorned with half-filled bowls of vibrant, freshly chopped vegetables, and scattered peels added a touch of charm amidst the organized chaos.

In the background, an old song's playlist filled the air, creating a nostalgic atmosphere that added an extra touch of magic to the moment.

"Please excuse the mess," Her voice was laced with endearing sincerity.

I softly chuckled, "If you call this a mess, you should see me attempt to boil water in the kitchen. My mom always teased me and said I could bring an earthquake just by entering!"

Her smile grew wider, filling the room with an enchanting glow as she gracefully approached the chopping counter. I stood near the fridge, captivated by her every movement as she skillfully battled with the tears brought on by the pungent onions.

I took a step towards her,

"Hey, please let me take care of this. I can chop. Trust me, you won't regret it," I gently insisted.

She peered into my eyes, a spark of gratitude igniting within her gaze, and reluctantly handed over the onions.

"You know, this step of cooking has always been my Achilles' heel. I struggle with them every time. Sorry, again," she became nervous.

I couldn't help but find her formalities endearing as our conversation evolved into laughter and a deepening connection. Time seemed to stand still as we reveled in one another's presence.

Suddenly, curiosity overcame me, and I couldn't resist asking,

"Hey, Tara, do your parents live in Mumbai? You must have missed them."

Her fading smile revealed a touch of melancholy as she responded, "Actually, Neil, my parents are divorced. My mom resides in Mumbai, while my dad is in Delhi."

My heart ached, and I expressed my sympathies,

"I'm so sorry to hear that. I had no idea."

At that moment, I realized the complexity that lay hidden beneath Tara's ever-present smile and boundless happiness. Determined to lighten the atmosphere, I regaled her with a humorous anecdote from my kitchen adventures.

"Tara, you know whenever I attempt to cook, I have a knack for dropping things so frequently that my mom used to say, 'If Newton had missed the apple that day, you would have redefined gravity by now.'" I burst into laughter, hoping to infuse some levity into the air.

She giggled, her voice filled with genuine warmth, "Your mom seems to be so cool, Neil. I never had the opportunity to live with mine during my childhood. Instead, I would watch other children playfully bantering with their mothers, and I was just happy witnessing their bond. I never truly experienced that cherished mother-daughter relationship that everyone speaks of. However, I do have a younger sister named Arya. We are each other's lifelines."

An indescribable tenderness washed over me as I detected a trace of sorrow in her expressive eyes. Seeking to alleviate her pain, I playfully dropped a few onions, purposefully pretending to be clumsy.

"See, I told you, I drop things like it's second nature," I interjected, hoping to bring back her smile.

With a peal of musical laughter, she playfully continued, "Ah, I see you're quite the physics enthusiast. Close your eyes, and let me impart you a little physics lesson today."

I couldn't help but respond,

"What? Close my eyes? Okay, I'm intrigued."

Following her request, I closed my eyes with a mixture of confusion and a subtle smile. She extended her hand, gently opening her fist, and a delicate shower of flour cascaded towards me, accompanied by her words,

"Behold, this is Newton's yet another law of physics..."

"Oh, I'm sorry...Neil, I am so sorry," she apologized, her voice filled with genuine concern.

In an unexpected twist, it was my impatience that led me to open my eyes prematurely, causing a bit of flour to find its way into my eyes. Though caught off guard, I assured her,

"Hey, it's okay. I'll be fine. Nothing serious." I chuckled, trying to put her at ease.

She was still worried, unable to shake off her feelings of guilt. Taking charge, she gently held my hand and guided me to sit on a nearby counter stool.

"Stay here, I'll get a damp cloth."

As she attended to me, her caring nature enveloped me, creating a sensation I had never experienced before. It was as if butterflies had taken up residence in my stomach, reminding me that someone out there cared for me in such a profound way.

Despite my attempts to resist, her unwavering concern broke through my defenses.

She returned, tenderly holding a damp tissue, and asked me to remain still. At that moment, she neared me without realizing the proximity between us. I could feel her breath gently brushing against my nose. Completely absorbed in her task, she became lost in the delicate process of cleaning my eyes, continually repeating how sorry she was.

My body trembled uncontrollably, overcome by the proximity we shared. I felt the stirring of something inside, a deep connection forming within me. But, at that moment, I managed to divert my thoughts, escaping the whirlwind of emotions that threatened to consume me.

In the background, a melodic tune began to play softly, the heartfelt lyrics of "Keh Du Tumhe....Ya chup rahu..." resonating through the air.

As the song filled the room, it struck a chord deep within me, stirring emotions that I had been unaware of until that very moment. Confused yet captivated, I couldn't help but wonder what this unfamiliar yet powerful feeling was that had taken root in my heart.

As she closely attended to my eyes, I could feel her warmth seeping into my skin, and her eyes spoke volumes of sadness and regret. She cast a compassionate gaze upon me, a mixture of relief and concern evident in her eyes as I managed to open my eyes properly, even though they were slightly reddened by the flour.

Her hands trembled ever so slightly as she held the damp tissue. At that moment, I reached out and gently pressed her palm, assuring her,

"Hey, it's okay. Don't worry. It's just plain flour that hit, not something as spicy as chili powder. I appreciate that you weren't attempting to teach me physics with a fiery twist." A warm smile adorned my face, attempting to put her at ease.

My tender touch seemed to affect her, and she too appeared slightly shaken yet wore a smile in response to my lighthearted comment. I motioned for her to sit beside me on the other stool, urging her to take a deep breath.

However, as fate would have it, the doorbell suddenly rang, causing us to both spring off the stools. We both knew it was likely Kabir and Kayla at the door.

The dinner preparations were nearly complete as Tara expertly wrapped up in the kitchen, while I set the table with care. The sound of Kabir and Kayla's playful giggles and teasing filled the air, adding a lightheartedness to the atmosphere.

Finally, after a while, we all gathered around the table. The melodious music continued to play softly in the background, enhancing the romantic ambiance. Kabir had brought a bottle of wine, which I promptly poured into three glasses. As for Tara, I filled her glass with coke.

Kayla's hunger got the better of her, and she expressed it with playful impatience, "I'm so hungry that I could eat you guys! Please, let's hurry up and start eating!"

Laughter filled the room as everyone engaged in lively conversation. Meanwhile, I found myself getting lost in the moment, surrendering to the magic of the evening.

Tara sat next to me, her eyes glistening with radiance. Her hair, slightly tousled from her time in the kitchen, was tied up in a long ponytail. Despite her efforts, a few baby hairs danced freely upon her forehead. Occasionally, as she moved, her messy braid would delicately brush against her hands, adding to her allure.

In that moment, the world seemed to fade away, leaving only the two of us, engrossed in each other's presence.

"Oh my goodness, Tara, your hands possess such charms," Kayla was unable to contain her admiration as we all savored the delectable meals cooked with love by her. In a playful jest, Kayla turned to me,

"Neil, would you please kiss her fingers for me? After all, you are right beside her."

At first, shock coursed through me, but it quickly transformed into laughter as the entire room erupted in mirth. Tara, initially bashful at the comment, soon found comfort in the shared laughter, feeling at ease within the warmth of the moment.

Our dinner was a true delight and, truthfully, As I indulged in each tantalizing morsel, a wave of adoration swept over me. The flavors danced upon my taste buds, igniting a passionate affair between my senses and the exquisite cuisine.

Yet, deep within my heart, a question lingered. Was it truly the food that had captivated me, or was there something more? Perhaps, hidden beneath the layers of flavors and textures, there lay an invisible thread connecting me to the person who had cooked this masterpiece.

At that moment, as I savored the lingering taste on my lips, I knew that this love was far more than just a gastronomic infatuation. It was a connection that transcended the realms of flavors and nourishment.

Following the meal, Kabir adjusted the volume of the music and settled onto the couch with Kayla. They delved into lively discussions about wedding attire choices and venue details, eagerly planning their future together.

Tara gracefully stepped into her role of post-dinner kitchen management, intending to carry out her tasks alone. Although she encouraged me to join Kabir and Kayla in the living room, my heart resisted.

I followed Tara into the kitchen, determined to offer my help.

"Today, I tasted the most exquisite meal of my life, Thank you". My voice was tender.

She responded with a soft smile, her cheeks tinted with a hint of shyness, before turning her attention back to her tasks, gracefully winding up the kitchen. I helped her in cleaning up the table and did little tasks just so I could spend a few more moments in her presence.

After some time, we re-emerged into the living room, joining Kabir and Kayla, who were absorbed in their conversation and held one another's hands tenderly. Kayla's glowing happiness was evident to us.

Tara lovingly poured more wine into our glasses, Kabir rose from his seat and invited Kayla to sway to the music playing in the background, -

"Hum tere bin ab nahi reh sakte......" its melodic notes fill the air.

As she exclaimed with joy and surprise, "Dance right here?" Kabir replied with absolute certainty, "Why not, baby? Come on."

Tara heightened the volume of the music, filling the room with its captivating rhythm, as she cheered on the couple.

A sudden rush of excitement swept over us as Kayla grabbed my hand and led me towards Tara. With a mischievous smile, she gently placed Tara's delicate hands in mine, urging us to embrace the music and dance together.

Tara and I exchanged glances, caught off guard by Kayla's unexpected move. Our eyes mirrored the confusion that filled the air, as we stood there, unable to comprehend what was happening.

Kayla, undeterred by our bewilderment, spoke up once more, her voice filled with encouragement, "Come on, you two. Don't be so formal, guys."

Kabir, joining in the playful persuasion, chimed in, his eyes filled with love, "Hurry up, buddy. Let's make some memories permanent."

As Tara and I continued to gaze into each other's eyes, we felt a tremor of uncertainty flutter in our hearts. It was clear that Tara was taken aback, her eyes revealing a touch of unease. We both seemed lost and unsure of how to respond.

In that delicate moment, I mustered the courage to approach Tara, tenderly clasping her quivering hands within mine. As I peered into the depths of her eyes, I sensed her attempt to decipher my intentions. Her gaze intermittently shifted downwards, and I could perceive the confusion hiding behind her nervousness.

Her vulnerability was evident, her heart beating in sync with mine. I, too, felt a mixture of excitement and hope, something at that point gave me the strength to carry us through the dance.

With every step we took, I guided her with gentle precision, my touch conveying unwavering support and understanding. I wanted to create an environment where she could let go of her fears and surrender to the magic of the moment.

I could feel our connection deepening with each synchronized step as if our souls were entwined in a dance of their own. Our eyes never wavered, locked in a shared expression of trust. I silently encouraged her, a soft smile playing on my lips, conveying my belief in her as we moved in harmony.

Tara's nerves slowly gave way to the sheer joy and beauty of the moment. A radiant smile bloomed on her face, illuminating the entire room. Her gaze shifted from the floor to me, still trying to read my eyes and vulnerability in my touch.

Together, we glided across the floor, lost in the music, oblivious to the surrounding world. It was a tender dance, filled with unspoken promises and whispered desires. In that intimate space, I pulled Tara a little closer, cherishing each precious moment.

With a soft touch, I gently guided Tara to a gentler pace, creating an opportunity for her to catch her breath. Our steps slowed, mirroring the thoughts racing through my mind. It was as if I could hear Kabir's silent inquiry, his cautious observation of our dance, and the emotions it created.

As the music swirled around us, Kayla's dancing came to a halt, her breathlessness evident in her voice as she turned to us and whispered, "Where is the water, Tara? I'm quite parched."

Suddenly, Tara's attention shifted, her hands pulling away from mine effortlessly as if realizing her neglectfulness. With a sense of urgency, she hurried towards the kitchen to fetch water for Kayla.

In her swift return, I witnessed a peculiar shift in Tara's demeanor. Her gaze averted from mine as if attempting to evade my eyes, a subtle unease lingering in the air.

As Tara busied herself by fetching wine, a glance at the clock sent a wave of realization crashing over me. It was already 1 a.m., the late hour punctuated by the soft ticking of the timepiece. A realization dawned upon me - it was time for me to leave.

With a gentle determination, I rose from my seat and made my way toward the kitchen, where Tara was pouring wine for Kabir and Kayla. I approached her softly, my voice laced with a hint of regret as I mentioned, "It's late, and I believe it's time for me to leave.

Her eyes held a playful glimmer as she met my gaze, her smile radiating warmth and affection. With a tender tone, she spoke, "It's the weekend tomorrow, Besides, Kabir and Kayla are already here. If you'd like, you can stay longer."

There was an underlying hint of effort in her voice, as she avoided direct eye contact. Perhaps, we had already exchanged our fair share of intense gazes during our dance, and now she sought to create a sense of comfort and distance.

Her invitation, though laced with a touch of hesitation, was a window into the depth of our connection. It signaled a desire to prolong the moments we shared, to revel in the motion of the present. And yet, I couldn't help but sense the gentle caution, as if she were guarding her emotions and cautiously navigating the fragile line between friendship and something more.

As much as every fiber of my being yearned to stay longer, I exercised restraint,

"I would love to, Tara, perhaps next time. But tomorrow morning, I must seize the early hours for the gym".

Her smile remained intact, a glimmer of understanding dancing in her eyes as she nodded in agreement.

"I genuinely enjoyed your company tonight, Neil," her voice was filled with gratitude. "It truly was an amazing evening. Thank you for being here."

With a bittersweet pang in my heart, I bid farewell to Kabir and Kayla, who were planning to spend the night, having indulged in a few too many drinks. Stepping out into the night, Tara followed me, our footsteps echoing in the quietude of the night. We exchanged our goodnights, a lingering connection woven in our gazes.

As I climbed into my car, the engine purring to life, my thoughts became a swirling whirlwind. The entire evening played on repeat in my mind, each memory etching itself deeper into my consciousness. I couldn't shake the haunting sensation of Tara's touch, the intensity of her gaze, the captivating beauty that seemed to radiate from her very essence.

Her delicate nature, her enchanting smile, and her mere presence engulfed my thoughts.

In that moment, a strange twist of longing tugged at my heartstrings, as I drove away from her, the distance between us growing with each passing moment. A whisper of the unknown echoed in my soul, leaving me craving for more, yearning for the day when our paths would cross again and the flame of unspoken desires would burn brighter.

After an intense workout in the gym, I felt the exhilarating rush of endorphins and the satisfying exhaustion that comes from pushing one's physical limits. My body was drenched in sweat, and my muscles were pleasantly fatigued, a testament to the effort I had put in during the session.

The combination of physical exertion and the sense of accomplishment left me feeling invigorated and ready to take on the day.

As I glanced at my phone, I realized I had missed a call from Maasi. Curiosity piqued, I quickly checked my messages and read her heartfelt words, "Neil, Beta... Mom has not been keeping well. She would be happy if you could come and spend a few days with her. She misses you dearly."

Without a second thought, I made up my mind and decided to drive to Jodhpur, Maasi's place. Along the way, I attempted to call my mom, but she didn't answer.

Finally arriving at my childhood home, I spotted my mom sitting on the beautifully lush lawn, engrossed in a book. Her eyes lit up with sheer delight as soon as she noticed my presence. Without hesitation, she rushed towards me, enveloping me in a warm and loving embrace.

Deeply touched, I respectfully touched her feet before settling down on a chair beside her. Her eyes glistened with tears of joy as she expressed how much she had missed me.

We spent a significant amount of time catching up, with my mom inquiring about my work and the office. She asked about Kabir and Kayla, showing genuine interest in their well-being. And as expected, she couldn't resist asking once again, "When will you get married, beta?" Though I chose to ignore that particular question, I assured her that I would soon return after freshening up.

Maasi, ever the thoughtful host, had set a grand dining table for us. Her skilled cooks had prepared a delicious feast that surpassed mere sustenance. We all gathered together, creating a vibrant atmosphere filled with laughter, heartfelt conversations, and an unwavering sense of togetherness. In those beautiful moments, we embraced the joy and warmth of being surrounded by loved ones, cherishing every interaction as a priceless treasure.

Afterward, I decided to take a nap, feeling a bit tired from all the travel. Just as I closed my eyes, a message from Tara popped up on my phone. She said, "Hey, what's up? Kabir and Kayla just left. He mentioned earlier that you're heading to your Mom's. Wishing her a speedy recovery. Take care and see you soon."

Tara always knew how to make others feel loved and cared for. The moment her message appeared, her face flashed in my mind.

It's strange, but thinking about her gives me this indescribable sensation that runs down my spine. I typed a simple message, "Sure, thanks. You take care too."

I shut my eyes, hoping to drift off into a peaceful sleep.

After what felt like a long nap, I woke up and made my way into the living room. Mom and Maasi were engrossed in conversation. When they noticed me, they gestured for me to join them on the couch.

Feeling groggy from the late-night escapades and early morning workout, I plopped myself down, resting my head on Mom's lap. I closed my eyes once again, knowing deep down that something had changed inside me. I couldn't quite put my finger on the details yet. Mom lovingly stroked my hair, and I slipped back into dreamland.

When I finally woke up, it was almost evening. I noticed that my phone had died, probably because I forgot to charge it. I rushed to plug it in and grabbed my laptop, attempting to focus on work.

After enjoying a satisfying dinner, I decided to play a playlist on Spotify and soak in the moment. Music has a way of connecting with memories, you know?

I ended up staying in Jodhpur for a good week. Mom and Maasi made sure I felt completely at ease and relaxed. I even asked Mom to come back with me, but she declined, "Beta, I know you need to focus on work right now. I'm quite settled here, but I'll visit you soon, don't you worry."

After bidding my farewells to everyone, I hit the road and made my way back to Gurgaon, the city known for its towering skyscrapers. The drive was filled with a sense of happiness, knowing that I had the chance to reconnect with my friends.

Upon arriving back, it was around 3 PM. Without wasting any time, I decided to head straight to the office. I could feel the excitement building up within me. It had been quite some time since I took a break of this length from work.

As I entered the office, Ana greeted me with a big smile. She seemed genuinely happy to see me after such a long hiatus. She followed me to my office, carrying a stack of files in her arms.

Kabir joined us, "Bhai, how's Mom?"

"She's doing better now." I felt content

"That's great to hear. Everything is being taken care of, so just relax a bit," Kabir assured me, before stepping outside to take a phone call.

With Kabir's comforting words in mind, I settled into my office and prepared to dive back into work. It felt good to be back in the rhythm of things.

At around 5 p.m., I left the office and headed home. Life seemed to fall back into its usual routine, except for one thing – our lunch schedules. Kabir was busy with work and preparations for his upcoming wedding. As for Tara, I hadn't heard from her and didn't feel like contacting her just yet. Some feelings needed to be sorted out before facing her.

Around ten days had passed, and the schedule was as packed as ever. However, one thing remained constant – there was no sign of Tara in the office or any messages from her.

I called Tara, but she didn't pick up. A growing sense of worry began to envelop me.

I called Kabir to see if he knew anything. Unfortunately, he had no news either.

I immediately called Ashok to bring the car around. Without wasting any more time, I left the office and rushed to Tara's home.

10 Ten

Upon reaching her doorstep, I pressed the doorbell. After a couple of seconds, a girl named Geeta answered the door. She seemed to recognize me from somewhere. She kindly invited me inside.

I sounded concerned, "Where is Tara?"

"She is sleeping, not keeping well for the past few days." She sounded nervous.

"Did she take medicines?" I was anxious.

"Yes, but her fever is not coming down." She added while offering me a glass of water.

After contemplating for a few minutes, I asked her to take me to Tara's room. Geeta hesitated for a moment, but eventually agreed and asked me to follow her.

We entered Tara's room, which was dimly lit with closed blinds. Geeta seemed unsure if she had made the right decision, and I couldn't help but question myself as well. However, I knew I had no other choice.

Approaching the bed, I saw that Tara was fast asleep. I gently touched her forehead and realized it was burning hot, with a temperature of around 103 degrees Fahrenheit. Uncertain of what to do, I asked Geeta to fetch a bowl of water and a clean cloth.

Geeta returned promptly with the items, and I settled down beside Tara, closer to her face. Her hands and feet were shivering. I held her fingers to keep them warm. She opened her eyes a little but felt helpless to say anything.

I began placing wet towels on her forehead, following a practice Mom used to do when I had a high fever.

Geeta assisted me as we tended to Tara. After about 20 minutes, her temperature started to cool down. Even in her half-asleep state, she muttered, "Neil.....?"

I whispered in her ears, "Hey!!!..."

Her eyes flickered open as if a surge of energy passed through her. She appeared incredibly weak. She tried to sit up on the bed, I held her hands firmly, reassuring her to stay lying down. "Please don't...," I gently urged her.

Feeling helpless, Tara complied and reclined on the bed, her gaze fixed on me. She couldn't say anything at that moment. Geeta finally left the room, convinced that she had made the right choice by allowing a stranger into their home.

Tara closed her eyes again, and I continued holding her hands, which were shaking. I could sense her entire body trembling. I pulled the quilt over her, ensuring she was tucked in properly. She spoke in a low, feeble voice, "When did you come back....?"

"Shhhhhh... Take a rest. No questions right now," I interrupted her softly.

"Just try to sleep. Don't worry, I'm here," I added, hoping to offer her some comfort and reassurance in that moment.

Tara drifted back into sleep, still holding onto my hand. I remained seated in the chair, silencing my phone and watching her peaceful slumber. In the meantime, Geeta had kindly made me some coffee, and I ended up drinking two cups in a row.

Tara slept undisturbed for about three hours, her temperature gradually cooling down and her discomfort subsiding. When she finally woke up, she opened her eyes and released my hand, a glimpse of guilt evident in her gaze.

I offered her some water, and she spoke with a trembling voice, "Neil... You've been sitting here for so long... I'm so sorry, I didn't realize I was holding onto you for that long."

"It's all right, How are you feeling now?" I asked her softly, concern evident in my voice.

"Let me take you to the doctor, or I can even arrange for a home visit," I offered, wanting to ensure she received proper medical attention.

"No... I'm feeling much better now. How are you? When did you come here? Sorry, I dozed off. How is your Mom?" Tara responded, her voice still trembling.

Hearing her voice again after such a long time brought me a sense of relief.

I asked Geeta to prepare some soup for her. Tara appeared hesitant and reluctant to eat, her appetite seemingly overshadowed by her physical state.

With a gentle and caring touch, I filled a spoon and carefully brought it to Tara's mouth, encouraging her to take a bite despite her trepidation.

She gazed at me, her eyes conveying a multitude of emotions, Tara gradually overcame her reluctance and took a few spoonfuls of soup.

I gave her the prescribed medicines, and gently touched her head to confirm that her temperature had improved. I tried to make her feel at ease,

"Hey, Try to catch some more sleep, okay?"

She reclined back and closed her eyes.

I observed her when she settled back into sleep, a sense of relief washing over me. After about an hour, I checked her temperature, it was getting better.

I glanced at the time on my phone, which read 11 p.m. With a heavy heart, I rose from my seat, provided a few instructions to Geeta to look after Tara, and left, hoping for her swift recovery.

11

♥Eleven

The next day, during my commute to the office, I decided to reach out to Tara, but she didn't answer her phone.

As I settled into work at the office, engrossed in my laptop, I heard a knock at my office door.

Startled, I looked up to find Tara standing there, a smile on her face. However, beneath that smile, I could still perceive a hint of lingering weakness in her eyes.

I jumped off from my chair, a mix of surprise and delight washing over me,

"Hey, How are you feeling?"

"Why aren't you at home, resting?"

"Please, Come and have a seat."

With a mysterious smile adorning her face, she entered my office, leaving me intrigued by the enigmatic aura that surrounded her.

"I'm fine, Neil."

"I wanted to say thanks for being there last night." Her words carried a touch of gratitude and sincerity.

I could still sense a hint of tremor in her voice.

After a brief catch-up, Tara took her leave and I returned to the task of preparing for the upcoming schedules of the day, and life resumed its normal rhythm.

Days passed by, our lunch dates resumed their familiar routine, and it wasn't long before the laughter and camaraderie returned. It was once again the four of us- Kabir, Tara, and occasionally Kayla- who gathered to share conversations, laughter, and the joy of life, mending the bonds of friendship and relishing each other's company.

As time passed by, my heart found itself increasingly drawn to Tara, and the bond between us deepened with each passing day.

One fine day, as we concluded our lunch, Kabir's face lit up with excitement as he enthusiastically announced that he was planning a pre-wedding party for the following day. This came as no surprise, as Kabir had a knack for finding reasons to celebrate and throw parties.

With the upcoming destination wedding in Goa on our minds, Tara and I shared a knowing glance and made a silent promise to attend Kabir's pre-wedding party the next night.

After our lunch, we parted ways, returning to our respective offices and the familiar rhythms of our daily routines.

The anticipated day arrived, and we made preparations for Kabir's grand pre-wedding party. It was not a small gathering by any means; instead, it was a lavish celebration set to be attended by our Stanford friends as well as our childhood buddies, promising a night of joyous reunion and revelry.

The pressure to choose the perfect outfit for such a significant occasion, coupled with my desire to look my best on my best friend's day, weighed heavily on my mind.

After considerable contemplation, I settled on wearing a Beige shirt with neatly folded sleeves, paired with a well-fitted pair of denim jeans.

Upon my timely arrival at the venue, I was greeted by the breathtaking sight of the celebration that Kabir had meticulously organized. With a heart full of appreciation, I ventured inside.

As a mark of respect, I first greeted and touched the feet of Kabir's parents, acknowledging their presence and seeking their blessings before moving further into the festivities.

Despite the crowd, I managed to locate Kabir and Kayla in the center of the hall, busy welcoming and mingling with the guests. However, I chose to divert my path and stepped onto the outdoor lawn.

While scrolling through my phone, I suddenly caught sight of Tara. She looked stunning, gracefully draped in a red saree with her hair left open. She adorned herself with a sleek diamond necklace and big earrings, a sight I had never seen before.

She stood on the lawn, holding a glass of mocktail, and we shared a big smile. I approached her, finding her standing alone with her phone.

"Hey, someone is looking amazing," I said in a friendly tone.

"Oh yes... I can see that," she replied, glancing at me mischievously.

Lately, I had been struggling to feel normal in front of Tara. But I always tried my best. One thing I noticed was that she had started reading my eyes thoroughly in any conversation.

Engaged in lightheaded chitchat, we began to savor the vibrant atmosphere and relish the joyous surroundings, immersing ourselves in the warmth of the gathering.

After some time, Kabir and Kayla made their grand entrance, accompanied by a lively group of friends,

"Hey guys!" all said in unison.

These were some of our cherished old friends and classmates, many of whom had gone on to become CEOs and entrepreneurs. As the introductions commenced, Tara was warmly presented to everyone, welcoming her into our tight-knit circle of friends with open arms.

Amidst the cheerful reunions and conversations, our focus shifted to the upcoming plans and schedules for Kabir and Kayla's upcoming wedding in Goa. With the flight scheduled for the day after, we discussed the details and shared our excitement for the destination wedding, looking forward to being part of their joyous celebration.

Amol, a friend from our Stanford days, playfully tapped my back and exclaimed,

"Dude, You lost the bet."

The unexpected revelation caught me by surprise, and I exchanged a bewildered glance with Kabir as we wondered about the nature of this bet and its outcome.

Amol went on to clarify, "Yes, Back in college, you embarrassed me in front of my then-girlfriend, and we made a bet which you've now officially lost," Amol explained.

I was still clueless. Kabir intervened, "Hey, bro, leave it... we were all drunk, and Neil wasn't even serious."

Amol laughed, "When you were making the bet, it seemed damn serious."

Tara listened to the conversation as clueless as I did.

Kayla intervened with a playful yet firm tone,

"Alright folks, Let's not bring any unnecessary drama into today's celebration. All family and relatives are here."

Kabir took charge and began to shed light on the situation, providing some context. He recounted,

"Back in college, Amol had a habit of changing his girlfriends almost every week. One night, we were quite inebriated, and Amol and Neil got into a heated argument. Neil wasn't pleased with Amol's revolving-door approach to relationships and commented in front of Amol's then-girlfriend. This led to a significant altercation, and in the aftermath, Amol challenged Neil that he needed to be either married, engaged, or at the very least, have a girlfriend by the time the last one of us got married."

Kabir's explanation brought the past bet into focus, providing a clearer understanding of the situation.

Amol looked at Neil,

"Dude, making bets and promises is one thing, but living life is another, which you have no idea about. You can't even find a girl, and yet you dared to challenge us. Now all of us are either married or in committed relationships except you. You only know how to make money and have no fucking idea of how to make real bonds or in other words 'Being Human'".

Amol started to get angry.

"Now, you have to do as we agreed upon. Get out a check and make sure it's a blank one."

I remained perplexed, my memory failing to recall the specifics of that particular day's bet or conversation. The entire situation had taken me by surprise, leaving me in a state of confusion as I attempted to piece together the details of our college days that had long faded into the past.

Amol continued to mock me, persistently asking for the checkbook.

Kabir once again intervened,

"Hey, relax bro. It's not a big deal."

Amol's behavior left us questioning whether he was either exceptionally intoxicated or had temporarily lost his sense of reason.

Kabir Leaned in towards Tara and whispered something into her ear. Her eyes, which had previously been filled with joy and anticipation, now flashed with a mix of nervousness and fear.

Kabir addressed the group with a mischievous twinkle in his eye and said,

"Folks, this isn't just about the bet. Who said Neil doesn't have a girlfriend?"

I gazed at Kabir, taken aback by his words. Without missing a beat, Kabir continued,

"Allow me to introduce you to Tara, Neil's girlfriend." His announcement seemed to leave the group pleasantly surprised and filled with happiness.

The revelation left everyone, including myself and Kayla, in a state of shock. Tara, too, appeared anxious, her unease evident in her posture as she looked down, her body and language betraying her nervousness amidst the surprised reactions of the group.

I and Kayla turned to look at Kabir, his statement had caught us completely off guard.

Tara made an effort to maintain a facade of normalcy and engage in conversation with everyone, but I could sense the underlying tension.

However, at that moment, all I wanted to do was punch Kabir in his face. How could he...? It seems like he never uses his brain. I was filled with frustration at the moment.

Amol came over to me with a smile, "Everything alright, bro? Chill. By the way, Congratulations."

A wave of anger surged within me, my emotions running high in response to the situation and the unexpected move by Kabir.

Overwhelmed by anger, I tightly clutched Tara's hand and swiftly led her away from the gathering. In my frustration, I held her hand so firmly that it bordered on causing her physical pain.

Tara's pleas echoed in my ears as she implored,

"Neil, please let go, you're hurting me"

She followed me through the hall, with Kabir and Kayla in close pursuit, desperately trying to catch up to my abrupt departure. Their faces were etched with concern and confusion.

I carried Tara to the empty terrace, my anger reaching a boiling point, and I couldn't contain it any longer.

I Exploded, my words flowing like a torrent,

"How could you, Tara...?"

My anger burned intensely as I continued,

"How could you simply go along with his words so easily?"

My disappointment and irritation were evident in every word I uttered.

I gazed at her, my anger still raging, even as she cried profusely. Tears streamed down her face without respite, and her distress was tangible.

Despite her tears, my anger remained at an all-time high, the intensity of the situation preventing me from immediately softening my stance.

In that tense moment, Kabir and Kayla arrived on the terrace. Kabir's voice resonated with a mix of incredulity and anger as he shouted at me,

"Neil, Are you serious?"

His anger flared as he continued,

"How could you possibly hurt Tara like this?"

The situation had escalated to a point where emotions were running high, and Kabir's outburst reflected his deep concern for Tara's well-being.

Kayla, with a compassionate gesture, approached and enveloped Tara in a comforting hug. Tara, still in tears, leaned into the embrace, finding solace in her friend's support.

Kabir recognizing the need for privacy, asked Kayla to escort Tara to her room, providing her with a safe space to collect her emotions and find comfort after the distressing events that had transpired.

My frustration and confusion left me pacing back and forth, my thoughts in turmoil as I struggled to make sense of the situation. My agitation reached its peak, and I couldn't help but raise my voice in Kabir's direction, demanding answers,

"What was that statement in front of everyone?"

"How could you drag Tara into all this?"

Kabir, attempting to diffuse the situation and urging me to regain my composure, responded,

"Neil, come to my room first. We can talk there. You're not thinking right now."

His words held a note of concern, and he recognized the need for a calmer, private discussion.

I forcefully shrugged off his hand from my shoulder.

"Answer me, Kabir?"

"Listen, I'm sorry. I know I made a mistake, but I couldn't think of anything else. I couldn't bear to see your integrity and values being questioned," Kabir replied in a softer tone.

"I just asked Tara to play along for a while, that's it."

"And you both just have to act around them. Both of you have such strong chemistry, that no one can have any doubts. They will leave in 7 days, and then the two of you can go back to normal," he approached me.

Kabir called his assistant to bring some glasses of water to the terrace.

Both of us took a few sips to calm our nerves. He then continued, his tone filled with concern,

"Bro you need to come with me and apologize to Tara right away."

"You have hurt her deeply, Neil."

"What were you even thinking?"

His words carried a sense of urgency and emphasized the need for immediate reconciliation and understanding.

After approximately half an hour of introspection and conversation with Kabir, I finally snapped out of my anger and realized the weight of the guilt I carried for my hurtful behavior towards Tara.

The realization had a profound impact on me, prompting a deep sense of remorse and the desire to make amends.

Kabir led me to Kayla's room, where I found Tara still overwhelmed with tears.

Kabir and Kayla left us alone in the room, allowing us the space and privacy to address the situation.

Tara stood by the window, her back turned to me as she gazed outside. I mustered the courage to speak, took a deep breath and began,

"I am sorry, Tara...!"

I was at a loss for words, uncertain of how to console her. I recognized that my actions had been utterly inappropriate, and no apology could fully rectify the pain I had caused.

Tara remained silent, her gaze still fixed on the outside, tears still flowing down her cheeks, as we both grappled with the complex emotions of the moment.

I added, my voice filled with sincerity,

"Tara, Please forgive me. I am genuinely sorry."

"I know how much you despise dishonesty, and witnessing Kabir make you part of it pushed me over the edge."

Tara remained silent and didn't turn to face me, leaving the weight of the moment hanging heavily in the room.

I took a step closer and noticed the redness on her wrist, a painful reminder of my unintentional harm during our earlier encounter in the hall.

Gently, I held her hand, softly touched her bruised wrist, and planted a warm kiss on it.

My plea was filled with earnestness,

"Tara, please, look at me, or at least say something. Your silence is tormenting me.

Tara turned slightly to locate her phone, which was resting on the bed. She attempted to retrieve it and leave the room.

Determined to make amends, I held onto her hand, continuing,

"I made a mistake, Tara. I see that now. I'm truly sorry."

"I couldn't bear to see you drawn into an act just because of some random person." My voice quivered with the weight of my emotions.

Tara turned back, her teary eyes locking onto mine,

"It was never about money, Neil."

"They were challenging your essence. I've witnessed how you genuinely care for the people around you, how you love and embrace them unconditionally."

She continued, her voice trembling with sincerity,

"Even if you would have given the check, Neil, No amount of money could compare to the honesty and appreciation you deserve."

"I willingly agreed to play along when Kabir asked me to because you deserve it." her voice was still shaking.

"Goodbye, Neil." and walked away, leaving me with a profound sense of realization and gratitude for the depth of her understanding and the purity of her actions.

Overwhelmed by the realization of my mistakes and filled with deep regret for my behavior, I left the room.

Upon stepping outside, I encountered Kabir and Kayla waiting for me in the lobby.

Kabir conveyed the news,

"Tara has left the party, Neil."

The weight of my actions weighed heavily on me.

With good wishes to Kabir and Kayla, I made the choice to leave the party and head home.

My attempts to reach Tara proved futile as she didn't answer my calls or read my messages. Overwhelmed with guilt and despair, I returned home and sought solace in a glass of whiskey.

I couldn't escape the relentless cycle of self-reflection and remorse. Only one question was bothering me at the moment,

"How could I ever hurt her?"

Soaked in thoughts, I spent the entire night on the terrace, reclining on the couch and gazing up at the starry sky.

12

♥Twelve

The following morning, the gentle embrace of sunlight roused me from my restless slumber.

With a heavy head and heart burdened with regret, I tried to get ready for the office.

As I entered my cabin, I found Kabir already waiting for me inside.

I swiftly occupied a seat, my anxiety building as he delivered a piece of surprising news,

"Neil, I just received an email from Tara. She is leaving the job and going back to Mumbai."

I was caught off guard and couldn't help but exclaim, "Whattttt..?"

"Yes, she's not even coming to the wedding. Kayla talked to her, but she had made up her mind. Bro, I'm not able to understand anything. Tomorrow we have to leave for Goa. Her flight is tonight."

"Is she in the office?" I inquired urgently.

"Yes, she's finishing up some meetings with vendors, handing over work, then she'll leave," Kabir sounded nervous.

I left Kabir in my office and stormed off, my urgency driving me to Tara's office.

I barged into Tara's office while she was busy with some files, with her assistant noting down a few documents.

As soon as she saw me, her assistant stepped out. I promptly locked the door, drew the blinds, and approached her.

She sat at her desk, disconnecting a call, and her demeanor revealed a mix of surprise and apprehension upon seeing me there.

I showed her the email she had sent to Kabir, which outlined her intention to step down from her role at Wadia Industries,

"What does this mean, Tara?" My voice was firm, yet tender at the same time.

She responded with a soft tone,

"Neil, I was about to talk to you about this."

"I can't continue with my job here, so I'm going back to Mumbai." Her eyes were filled with guilt.

I walked up to her, gently holding her bruised wrist, and looked down at her red wrist before meeting her eyes. I managed to speak, albeit with difficulty,

"What about us, Tara?"

Unprepared for the question, she appeared taken aback and anxious. She peered into my eyes as if searching for something she needed to find within them.

"All right if that is what you want," I replied after a few seconds.

A single tear trickled down my cheek, a silent testament to the emotions I was struggling to contain,

"Just one favor, please," My voice quivered.

She looked up at me, her eyes were wet.

"Please stay until the wedding, Tara. Please, don't let Kabir and Kayla suffer the consequences of my actions. If you agree, we can maintain the facade of being a couple in front of everyone.", I implored,

" Or If it makes you more at ease, I won't even attend the wedding. But please, don't break their hearts because of me."

Tears welled up in her eyes and began to trickle down her cheeks.

I lightly pressed her hand, offering a gentle, reassuring touch, before swiftly leaving her office.

I made my way home, overwhelmed by the urge to unwind with a strong glass of whiskey and regain my composure.

I had spent the entire night on the terrace, a solitary company of whiskey on my table. I had even lost track of how many glasses I had emptied. The clock had cruelly ticked its way to 3 a.m. My head throbbed in agony, matching the relentless pounding of my heart. Regret consumed me gnawing at my conscience.

What have I done? I never meant to hurt her, never wished to let her slip away. Yet here I was, drowning in the overwhelming feeling of loss. She was leaving, and I had missed my chance to hold on. I felt utterly worthless, always watching those most precious to my heart slip through my fingers, leaving me empty and desolate.

I frantically reached for my phone, my heart pounding with hope that Tara had replied to my messages from the previous night, but the screen remained void of her response, leaving an ache in my chest that refused to dissipate.

Instead what met my eyes was a message from Kabir sent in the late hours of the night, a reminder of the impending departure, " The flight is early in the morning, Be ready at 5 AM. "

I closed my eyes with a heavy heart, a sense of unease washing over me. It felt as though my entire body trembled, uncertain whether it was due to the chili December breeze or the coldness of heart I displayed the previous night.

Tomorrow marks a significant day as we all embark on a journey to Goa for a destination wedding, a celebration of love that has blossomed and matured over time. My train of thought was abruptly detailed as my phone chimed with an incoming message. My heart raced as I hastily reached for it, and my hands turned cold as ice, while a chill ran down my spine.

Summoning every ounce of courage, I opened the message, my trembling fingers navigating through Tara's text,

"Hey, It will be great if we stick with the original plan to attend the wedding. I will also be there. We can keep up this charade for a week for Kabir and Kayla. and then we will go our separate ways. See you and take care, Neil".

The message left me in a whirlwind of emotions, a mix of relief and sorrow, as I grappled with the profound implications of what lay ahead.

It pierced through me like a cold, heartless dagger. Her words were devoid of warmth, so formal, and it tore at the very fabric of my being. The thought of feigning normalcy in front of everyone, when our hearts had drifted so far apart, was an unbearable weight on my soul.

Collecting every ounce of strength, I forced myself to rise from my seat, my heart heavy and my emotions turmoil. I hastily gathered my belongings and threw them into my bag, the rush of it mirroring the chaos within me.

In a flurry, I stepped into the shower, the cascading water offering me a brief, soothing respite from the tempest of emotions. With a racing heart and an unsettled mind, I rushed to the airport, the urgency of my departure matching the storm of feelings that churned inside.

As I made my way to the airport, the anticipation of seeing Tara weighed heavily on my heart. I couldn't help but feel a sense of trepidation, uncertain of how I could turn back time, to that very moment and correct the mistakes I had made.

My yearning to convey to her the depth of my feelings, to express just how much she meant to me, was overpowering. Emotions surged through me, making my hands tremble and my heart race, leaving me feeling incredibly vulnerable.

Tara's message, urging us to do the act of pretense in front of everyone, for the sake of not affecting the joyous union of Kabir and Kyla, further tugged at my emotions.

It was as though we were being asked to hide our own hearts' turmoil behind an act to protect the happiness of our dear friends. The weight of this responsibility was both an act of love and a painful burden on me.

13

♥Thirteen

As the clock struck 5 AM, I arrived at the airport, where a buzz of activity was already in full swing. Amol, a familiar face among the group, waved at me from a distance, and I reciprocated with a friendly gesture. Meanwhile, Kabir and Kayla, deeply engrossed in last-minute arrangements, were juggling myriad tasks.

I didn't hesitate to step in, lending a hand to them, managing luggage, and ensuring that everything was in order for the guests.

With the entire flight booked for their wedding festivities, the logistics of organizing such a large group at the airport were proving to be quite a task.

In the midst of all this, I spotted Tara sitting in the waiting lounge, engrossed in her diary, her thoughts edged upon the pages.

I approached her, and she looked up, her warm smile greeting me, "Hey, good morning."

I couldn't help but feel perplexed by her seemingly normal demeanor given the emotional turmoil of the past incidents. Nevertheless, I met her warm smile with equally tender words,

"Hey, How are you?" as we shared a moment that held so much unspoken meaning beneath the surface.

She seemed nervous and just nodded her head.

I continued, "Tara, everyone is gathering, Kabir and Kayla are waiting for us..." The unspoken current of our shared secret weighs heavily in the air, but for now, we would continue to play our parts in the unfolding drama of Kabir and Kaila's love story, as we agreed upon.

With a soft closing of her diary, Tara gracefully picked up her handbag, and we made our way toward the boarding gates. In the distance, Kabir and Kayla spotted us, their faces breaking into relieved smiles as they waved in acknowledgment of our presence.

Tara's demeanor seemed to defy the weight of the past night, as she skilfully maintained an air of normalcy. It was as if the storm that had swept through our lives had left no mark on her.

As Amol approached us, Tara's hands inched closer to mine, and our fingers brushed against each other, sending a subtle, electric jolt through my heart. Without a second thought, I gently clasped her hand and caressed the bruised wrist, the connection providing a sense of comfort in the midst of our shared secret.

Amol waved at us, his smile radiant, and he cheerfully declared, "There is my favorite couple," seemingly oblivious to the intricate dance of emotions that played out beneath the surface.

At that moment, the bustling sounds of travelers and the constant hum of announcements seemed to fade into the background as I reached out, my trembling fingers finding solace in the touch of her hand.

We continued walking, our clasped hands serving as a bridge, closing the distance between us. Even though I was aware that our interaction was merely a facade, the sheer proximity of being near her always brought me deep satisfaction.

During the flight, we ended up with seats next to each other. As we settled down, Kabir and Kayla were beaming with happiness, ready to take the first step of their life together. I offered the window seat to Tara. In a few seconds, we settled down there.

The atmosphere on the flight was palpably joyful, an effervescent celebration of love and togetherness that enveloped everyone on board. Laughter, Camaraderie, and warm conversations filled the air as we embarked on this momentous journey.

Yet, amidst the jubilation, an undercurrent of uncertainty tugged at my heart. I couldn't shake the unease that lingered within me, a cloud of doubt that cast a shadow over the sky of my unknown feelings arising somewhere in the middle of my heart.

I took a brief respite, closing my eyes for a moment to collect my thoughts. When I opened them, I found Tara deeply engrossed in her diary. Her pen danced gracefully across the pages, a testament to her diligence and the depths of her contemplation. Lost in her world, she seemed distant, her thoughts hidden behind the veil of her words.

The site of the red bruise on Tara's left wrist was like a searing brand of guilt, invoking an overwhelming wave of self-hatred within me. As the memories of the past incidents rushed back, I despised myself in that moment, grappling with the weight of my actions and their impact on Tara.

With a heart heavy with remorse, I cautiously extended my hand towards hers, tenderly clasping her fingers in my own. My touch was gentle as I began to softly caress her hand, a silent acknowledgment of the pain I had inflicted. Tara met my gaze briefly, her eyes a tempest of tears and raw emotions, before she lowered her head, the unspoken turmoil in her heart apparent.

I tried to speak, to express the depth of my regret, but the words seemed to become lodged in my throat, leaving us ensnared in a profound and heavy silence for what felt like an eternity. At last, I mustered the courage, "I'm genuinely sorry, Tara...!" My fingers continued to trace the contours of the bruise with the utmost care.

Tara's eyes remained fixed on the window, and a few tears traced silent paths down her cheeks. I continued to hold her hands, my touch a plea for her understanding and forgiveness. After a while, she gently withdrew her hands from my grasp, and looked over at me, her eyes filled with warmth and a hint of curiosity, before returning to her writing.

The pain of the previous night's events lingered in the air, and the unspoken words echoed in the quiet of our shared space.

With a heavy heart, I leaned back against the chair's headrest, seeking solace in the darkness behind closed eyelids. I tried to catch up on the much-needed rest that had eluded me. The gentle hum of the airplane and the comforting embrace of sleep became my refuge, offering a brief sanctuary amidst the storm of my emotions.

14

♥ Fourteen

After approximately 2.5 hours of flight, we finally landed in Goa. The excitement among everyone was palpable. Kayla's mother accompanied her, engaged in lively conversation and laughter, while Kayla himself hugged her in between.

Tara observed this heartwarming scene and smiled softly. I walked over to Kabir to help with the guests and their luggage, lending a hand wherever needed.

We all boarded taxis and made our way to the venue. Tara and I were in the same car. There was an undeniable awkwardness in the air, and Tara gazed out of the window, lost in her thoughts.

I focused on my laptop, typing away as the car cruised for approximately 70 minutes. Finally, we reached the venue, which was a magnificent resort overlooking the ocean, with direct access to the shoreline.

In the embrace of this coastal paradise, the tropical climate caresses your skin with gentle breezes, whispering secrets of the sea. It's a symphony of warmth and comfort, where the air carries the sweet scent of flowers and salty ocean mist, mingling in harmonious union.

Every moment exudes an air of romance, from the vibrant colors that paint the landscape to the rhythm of the waves crashing upon the shore. It is a destination where love and nature intertwine, creating an atmosphere that ignites the flames of passion and leaves an indelible imprint upon the soul. As soon as we arrived, Tara practically leaped out of the car as she caught sight of the vast ocean. A wave of happiness washed over me, witnessing her genuine excitement.

Love and joy filled the air as Kabir and Kayla embraced each other, making a heartfelt announcement, "Ladies and Gentlemen, welcome to 5 days of warm hospitality and celebration. We wish you a happy stay. You will be escorted to your respective rooms, where you will find a personalized itinerary that we highly recommend you follow to make your stay even more memorable. Love ya!"

An attendant approached Tara and me, offering a warm greeting before leading us to a grand suite with breathtaking views of the ocean.

The suite nestled by the ocean was a vision of pure luxury and tranquility. As you entered, you were immediately greeted by a sense of grandeur and elegance. The spacious layout allowed for a seamless flow between the different living areas, with ample room to relax and unwind.

Large windows adorned the walls, offering breathtaking panoramic views of the sparkling ocean waters.

The sight of the waves crashing against the shoreline created a mesmerizing display, inviting you to lose yourself in the beauty of nature.

The furnishings were chic and sophisticated, carefully selected to blend modern aesthetics with comfort. Plush sofas and armchairs beckoned you to sink in and bask in the panoramic vistas that surrounded you. The decor exuded a coastal charm, with soft hues and natural textures echoing the serenity of the ocean.

Moving towards the bedroom, you were greeted by a lavish king-sized bed adorned with the finest linens. The room was tastefully adorned with subtle touches of luxury, ensuring a peaceful night's sleep in the lap of opulence.

Stepping out onto the private balcony, you were greeted by a refreshing sea breeze, a gentle reminder of the natural wonder just beyond your doorstep. Here, you could relax in comfortable outdoor furniture while indulging in breathtaking sunsets or simply listening to the soothing sounds of the waves.

The en-suite bathroom was a sanctuary in itself, boasting a sleek design and modern amenities. A deep soaking tub beckoned to envelop you in tranquility, while a spacious walk-in shower offered a refreshing escape after a day spent exploring the resort.

Overall, this resort suite by the ocean was a haven of luxury and serenity, offering a truly remarkable experience for those seeking an indulgent getaway by the water's edge.

As Tara and I walked into the suite, she gazed at the plush bed, and then at me.

Without a second thought, I offered," Please take the bed, Tara. I'll take the couch." With that, I walked outside to the balcony, captivated by the stunning scenery that surrounded us.

Tara looked a bit confused, but she placed her handbag down and entered the washroom. After freshening up, she checked the itinerary that was provided in the room.

It indicated that we were free to relax or explore the property. High tea was arranged by the seaside at 5 p.m., providing the perfect opportunity to admire the sunset. At 9 p.m., after dinner, we were encouraged to gather around the bonfire and enjoy live music by the band.

Despite being confused at first, Tara soon relaxed and embraced the itinerary's plan, looking forward to the many wonderful experiences she would enjoy over the coming days.

As I entered the room, I noticed Tara sitting at the desk, deeply engrossed in writing something in her diary. In a hurry, I headed straight to the washroom to take a quick shower, eager to lend a hand with the preparations and arrangements being made by Kabir. Meanwhile, Tara continued to diligently pen her thoughts.

Around 4 p.m., I returned to find Tara sound asleep, peacefully resting on the bed.

The gentle breeze had caused her hair to fall across her face, causing some discomfort. I came close to her, Gently, I brushed the stray strands away before stepping out onto the balcony.

The azure waters extend as far as the eye can see, merging seamlessly with the expansive sky. The rhythmic dance of the waves captivates your senses, creating a serene symphony that fills the air.

You could hear the soothing melody of the waves crashing against the shore. The sound serves as a lullaby, gently lulling you into a state of tranquility, and creating an atmosphere of peace and harmony. The fresh ocean air invigorates your senses, carrying with it a hint of salt and the faint fragrance of sea life, reminding you of the vastness and beauty of the underwater world.

After about half an hour, I came back from the balcony. Tara was awake and greeted me with a warm smile.

I smiled back with an expression of guilt in my eyes. In this breathtaking atmosphere and scenic beauty, I felt like pouring my heart out to Tara but the thought just vanished in the sound of waves crashing against the beach.

I noticed that she had changed into a stunning white dress, making her look like an angel amidst the beautiful surroundings.

15 Fifteen

At around 5 p.m., we walked out of the room to join the others. Slowly, everyone congregated, and we embarked on a ten-minute stroll to the sunset point. As we walked, I tried to check the bruise on her wrist, which she tried to conceal with a matching pearl bracelet.

The thought started to gather in my mind," What will happen after 5 days once the facade is over?", "How I'm gonna live without her?" I wanted to hold her hand so badly, wanted to caress her wrist but somehow restrained myself.

Once we reached the sunset point, Kabir and Kayla eagerly greeted us. Kayla affectionately kissed Tara on the cheek and whispered, "Looking gorgeous babe," Tara smiled with a pinch of shyness across her cheeks.

They directed us to our table and began to leave, but Kayla returned, taking hold of Tara's hand while subtly brushing against mine, silently asking me to hold on. Tara glanced at her, and Kayla responded with a quiet reassurance, "Just for one week, baby, please."

Those last words struck a chord within me, but I maintained my poker face, concealing my true feelings as I always did.

I delicately held her hands, my touch gentle and caring as I caressed the bruised skin. Her gaze was fixed on the horizon, emanating an aura of calmness and serenity.

The horizon, where sky and sea intertwine, becomes a canvas for nature's paintbrush. Fiery hues of orange and pink transform the sky into a breathtaking masterpiece, as if the sun sets the heavens ablaze, casting a warm glow that envelops everything in its embrace.

The colors blend and mingle, creating a seamless transition from day to twilight, casting a spell of tranquility and serenity. In that moment, it became clear to me that these hands were the ones I wanted to hold forever, through every moment of our lives.

Tara, silent in her thoughts, sat beside me as the sun began its graceful descent. The view before us was nothing short of breathtaking – the sky painted a vibrant shade of red, the vast expanse of the ocean stretching out before our eyes. And beside me sat Tara, a dream come true, the embodiment of everything I could ever imagine.

From a distance, Kabir's gaze met mine, as though he had something important to convey without uttering a single word.

Just then, We saw Amol and his wife, Kriti approaching our table. Tara noticed their arrival and, with a gentle lean, rested her head against my chest. A shiver ran through me before I carefully enveloped her in a tender hug, effectively shielding her from any discomfort. At that moment, her eyes softly closed, and I watched over her with utmost tenderness.

Kriti, introduced herself to Tara with excitement, expressing her admiration as a devoted fan. She showered Tara with praise, commending her talent for weaving emotions through her words, and requested a picture together.

It was a revelation to me that Tara had a significant following on social media, and her books were widely celebrated as bestsellers. Although I had never read her books before, I knew it must have been extraordinary.

Kabir was coming towards me, he gently pulled me aside,

"Bro, Are you ever gonna tell her?"

I was taken aback by his words.

"The whole world can read your eyes, I am sure she also could."

"What are you scared of?"

As he continued to speak, his words seemingly fading into the background, I stood there in silence, my gaze fixed on Tara. She was a radiant presence, a vision of happiness and warmth as she mingled with her friends, her smile illuminating the air. I couldn't help but be captivated by the genuine joy that enveloped her, finding solace in the simple pleasure of witnessing her happiness.

"She deserves to know Bro." Kabir was still there.

With a pat on my back, Kabir left me standing there, deep in thought.

As I came back to the table, I was looking for the right moment, the perfect opportunity to express myself. She also returned to the table, her gaze now fixated on the sunset. I stood beside her, feeling a mix of nervousness and determination, ready to find the right words to convey my true feelings.

The sun was slowly going down with grace and beauty. Tara's eyes were filled with little tears which she was trying to hide from everyone. I held out my hand to ask for hers. She looked at me, tenderly held my hands, and again rested her head on my chest. A few tears rolled down her cheeks, I wiped her eyes softly with my fingers, caressed her hair a little, and embraced her smoothly.

She pressed her head against my chest, seeking comfort in the solace of our embrace. Gently, she rubbed her head against my shirt, a subtle and intimate gesture that conveyed a profound connection and a need for reassurance.

I pressed a soft, tender kiss on her forehead, a gesture meant to convey my love and care. In response, she shivered slightly, her emotions palpable. A few more tears welled up in her eyes, tracing a silent path down her cheeks and coming to rest on her chin, a testament to the depth of her feelings in that moment. Our silent exchange spoke volumes, a shared connection that transcended words.

Every inch of my body tingled as our fingers delicately intertwined. I couldn't help but wonder if this connection with Tara was genuine and if she truly desired to hold on to me. After all, she was "The Tara Patel."

We sat there for another thirty minutes, the tea in front of us growing cold, untouched. Neither of us was in the mood to indulge in it.

As the daylight retreats, the stars take their places, one by one, illuminating the night sky like glittering jewels. The moon, casting its gentle glow upon the water, creates a path of silver shimmering brilliance that seems to reach out and beckon you to embark on a romantic journey.

Our group slowly began to disperse, each person making their way back to their suites to prepare for dinner before the evening's bonfire. Kabir and Kayla, as always, were on top of the itinerary, ensuring we stayed on track.

I remained, gently caressing the fading bruise on Tara's wrist, a silent acknowledgment of the lingering pain etched into my heart.

Her eyes were closed, her thoughts concealed behind the veil of her emotions. Leaning in closer, I whispered in her ear, "Tara, Are you okay?". My words carried a mix of tenderness and genuine concern, a desire to bridge the emotional distance between us.

She shivered slightly, her eyes meeting mine as she offered a subtle nod in response. We finally made our way to our room.

16

♥Sixteen

After savoring the beauty of the sunset, we made our way back to our room. Tara's uncharacteristic silence hung in the air, a noticeable departure from her usual demeanor.

I contemplated breaking the silence with words of comfort, but uncertainty held me back, leaving me to wonder if this was the right time to address the unspoken thoughts between us.

To distract myself and give Tara some space, I turned to my laptop and immersed myself in work. An hour passed in the quiet hum of the room, but eventually, we received a call inviting us to join for dinner.

As we made our way to the dining area, I gently suggested to Tara that we dine by the ocean, hoping that a change of setting might help shift her mood.

The idea of dining by the ocean seemed to excite her, and before long, we were comfortably seated at a table near the water's edge.

Tara's choice for the evening was a simple tomato soup and some vegetables, while I ordered a small salad to accompany her. My appetite had waned, but being in her company was reason enough to partake in the meal, as the waves gently lapped at the shore, providing a soothing backdrop to our evening.

Our gazes met occasionally during the meal, but most of the time Tara was engrossed in her phone. In the glow of the screen, she radiated amidst the darkness. Her eyes seemed swollen and anxious.

As I sat across from Tara, I found myself entranced by her presence, feeling as though I could gaze into her eyes and lose myself in the depths of her soul for an eternity.

Just then, Kabir came looking for us, exclaiming, "There you are!"

“After dinner, we have to gather around as planned. See you guys later.” Tara and I both nodded in agreement, but she quickly returned her attention to her phone, while I retreated into my contemplative thoughts.

Once the waiter cleared our table, Tara put her phone away, and we made our way to the bonfire, following the itinerary.

As we approached the setup, the flames blazed brightly against the moonlit ocean, casting a warm, flickering glow on the surroundings. The crackling sounds of the fire filled the air, harmonizing with the scent of burning wood and the gentle sea breeze.

Seated close to the fire, we embraced its warmth, finding solace in the cool night air. The flames continued their dance, creating beautiful shadows that danced across our faces, adding an air of enchantment to the scene.

The crashing waves provided a soothing melody that blended with the crackling fire, creating a serene symphony that washed away our worries and filled us with tranquility.

Each wave seemed to synchronize with the rhythm of the bonfire, creating a perfect harmony that embraced our souls amidst the vastness of the beach.

Gazing into the depths of the fire, I couldn't help but feel captivated by its hypnotic allure. Sparks danced and spiraled into the sky, disappearing into the vast expanse above like fleeting shooting stars.

As the night deepened and the flames danced on, the bonfire became a beacon of warmth and connection. It brought people together, fostering bonds of friendship and kindling flames of passion in the hearts of lovers.

Summoning up my courage, I leaned in close to Tara's ear and whispered, "Tara..."

She gazed at me intently, her eyes conveying a depth of understanding that only I could hear. She nodded softly, silently encouraging me to continue.

"I have something to tell you," I said, my voice tender and vulnerable.

Once again, Tara looked at me, giving me a signal to proceed.

But just as the words formed in my mouth, Kayla approached us, whispering something in Tara's ear. I couldn't quite catch what she said, but I sensed that Kabir's name was mentioned.

Tara smiled and chuckled softly, while Kayla walked away laughing. A live band played soft songs, adding to the ambiance.

I searched for Tara's hand, caressing it gently. She glanced down briefly before fixing her gaze on the fire.

Looking at me, she asked with a tender voice, "Neil, What were you saying?"

At that moment, I lost my train of thought. I couldn't figure out what to say. I simply shrugged my shoulders and replied,

"Maybe later..."

Tara nodded and returned her gaze to the fire.

I berated myself for stifling the liveliest person on earth. Tara used to be a constant stream of chatter and laughter. And she is the quietest.

After a while, Kabir and Kayla joined us, their hands intertwined. We exchanged smiles as they gracefully began to dance together to the sweet melodies of the live band.

The song- "Mere Haath Mein...tera hath ho..." played, filling the air with its enchanting notes.

Kabir's handheld Kayla's as he gently guided her movements in perfect rhythm. He pulled her closer, planting a kiss on her cheek, his lips forming the words "I love you."

Something stirred within me. "Am I in love?" I wondered.

"Is this what I feel for Tara? Is this what love truly feels like?"

And so the never-ending chain of thoughts began once more...

Suddenly, I heard cheering and noticed Tara smiling. I looked again and saw Kabir standing in awe while Kayla knelt, offering him a rose and professing her love for him. Kabir embraced her tightly, both of them overcome with tears of joy.

I glanced at Tara, observing her joy in their happiness.

As the music played and everyone started dancing with the lovely couple, Kabir approached us and pulled us onto the dance floor. I held Tara's hand tightly, and then gently took her other hand as well. We started dancing slowly, and as I looked into Tara's eyes, I sensed that she was trying to decipher something.

A wave of fear washed over me. What if Kabir was right? What if Tara could see through my feelings too? I didn't want her to feel unsafe amidst all these overwhelming emotions.

Swiftly, I placed one of Tara's hands on my shoulder and rested my other hand on her waist. She continued to search my eyes, seeking something within them.

In her eyes and expressions, I noticed a tenderness that warmed my heart. We moved our bodies together, swaying slowly to the rhythm of the song,

"Main Aashiq Toh Nahi...magar ae haseen...." It felt as though love had taken hold of us.

Lost in the moment, Tara was still reading my eyes, following the lead. As the song ended, the room filled with applause and laughter. We stopped dancing and returned to our seats. Eventually, everyone started dispersing and heading to their rooms.

Softly, Tara asked me, "Would you mind if we go near the ocean, just once?"

I hesitated, concerned about the cold water, and replied, "Are you sure? It might be cold out there now."

"I know," she replied, "That's why I want to go."

17

♥Seventeen

With a nod, I followed Tara towards the ocean. The breeze grew colder as we approached, and though the darkness enveloped us, there was enough moonlight to see each other.

Tara gently released her hand from mine and walked right into the ocean. She stood at a certain point, fixated on the waves as they caressed her, sometimes even splashing up to touch her hands. Tara remained still, lost in the beauty of the scene before her.

Approaching her, I whispered, "It's high tide, Tara. I think you should step back a little."

She smiled and replied, "Neil, they won't harm me, ever. I am sure."

Her words hit me hard. I realized I had unintentionally hurt her deeply, and it felt like a shard piercing my heart to hear those words coming directly from her.

Tara continued, her voice filled with emotion,

"Do you know, Neil, back in Mumbai, when I used to feel alone, the ocean was my refuge? I could sit there for hours, with the waves embracing me again and again. It felt like they were hugging me, telling me to stop feeling lonely. It feels like home here."

I looked at her, a tear rolling down her cheek while she still smiled, mesmerized by the ocean's embrace.

A powerful urge coursed through me, compelling me to give her a tight hug, to reassure her that she was not alone and would never be. However, I resisted, not wanting to invade her personal space without her consent.

Tara stood there for around 20 minutes, immersed in the loving embrace of the ocean's waves.

Later, she took a step back and settled onto the soft sand. I joined her, feeling the chilly breeze against my exposed skin. Tara, in her sleeveless dress, seemed unaffected by the cold.

I, on the other hand, decided to remove my full-sleeved shirt to provide her with some warmth. I gently slid my arms around her, hoping to offer comfort and protection.

I was still clad in a half t-shirt, and she hesitated, saying, "I'm fine, Neil. It's okay."

Despite her resistance, I persisted, wrapping one arm around her and then the other. Her smile returned, and her attention drifted back to the vast ocean.

We sat there in silence for around 30 minutes, embracing the tranquility of the moment. Tara eventually reclined on the sand, as though she wanted to truly connect with the earth beneath her. Enchanted by the moonlight, I mimicked her actions and lay down beside her. Together, we gazed at the stars that adorned the darkened sky.

After a peaceful silence of 10 minutes, she broke it with an apology. "Neil, I'm sorry for that day. I shouldn't have lied in front of your friends."

Her words took me by surprise, and I locked eyes with her. She was already looking at me, waiting for a response.

"And also sorry for storming off later," she continued, not wanting me to interrupt.

Before I could say anything, she stopped me, pleading, "Please let me speak, Neil."

"I'm sorry for everything," she confessed.

"And Thank you for inviting me to the wedding. Without it, I would have missed out on feeling at home here."

Then, she fell silent for another 10 minutes. In that stillness, I took hold of her hand lying between us, gently pressing my palm against hers as our fingers intertwined.

After another pause, she began again, "Neil, the way you're caressing my bruise says a lot about you."

Curious, I asked,

"What does it say to you, Tara? Because to me, it's a reminder of how unworthy and selfish I am."

"You care for people, Neil," she replied with conviction. "And you never want to hurt them intentionally."

I glanced at her once again, and a single tear trailed down her cheek.

"I disagree, Tara. I can never forgive myself for hurting you," I confessed softly, my voice trembling with emotion.

"You know, Neil," she whispered, "you always ask me about the secret of my happiness."

I looked at her, eager to hear her answer.

"PAIN," she revealed. "I have experienced so much pain that now I remind myself to embrace happiness whenever I can."

Silence wrapped around us once more as we lay there, hand in hand, contemplating the complexities of our emotions in the stillness of the night.

"I want to smile in happiness, sadness, loneliness, and ever," she uttered.

I knew deep within that she was broken. Her eternal smile concealed her true emotions, but one thing was certain - I was lying next to the most intelligent and sensible girl in the world.

"When I was younger, my dad never allowed me to see my mom. I didn't lay eyes on her until I was around 5 or 6 years old. Whenever I asked about her, he would redirect my attention. As I started going to school, I observed other children giggling and teasing their mothers. I found joy in simply watching them. Sometimes, I would become so overwhelmed that I would cry and scream at home, longing to be with my mom. In response, I would be slapped to silence," she chuckled softly.

"Your dad hit you?" I exclaimed, my shock evident.

"That was the only way he could keep me quiet or divert my focus at that moment. Most of the time, it was just his hands, but he used a stick occasionally," she said softly.

I abruptly sat up, feeling as though crashing waves were about to engulf me. "What??" I asked anxiously.

"Are you serious, Baby? How can someone be so inhumane as to strike such a young child?" I questioned, anger coursing through me.

"One time, my dad wasn't at home, and my mom came to take me with her. He became so furious that he grabbed me by my wrists and forcefully dragged me to the car, and then from the car to our home," she disclosed tenderly.

I was already seated, but I sprang up, stepping back, feeling overwhelmed with anxiety.

"Oh my... what have I done?" I muttered.

Tara also stood back, moving closer to me. "I'm sorry, Neil. That day, I overreacted when you dragged me to the terrace. It was a painful reminder of my childhood, and I despise those experiences. My childhood holds no pleasant memories, Neil," she admitted.

"In that moment, the pain I felt was not just from the bruise, but from the emotional scars I carry due to my past. Please, stop blaming yourself for that day. It was not your fault," she held my hand.

Tears streamed down my face as I struggled to find a balance of thoughts. I didn't know what to do. Tara, too, was in tears. We moved closer to each other. I reached out and held her other hand.

In a broken voice, I whispered, "I'm truly sorry, Tara. I could never intentionally hurt you. Trust me. And I am so sorry for all the painful memories you've carried from your childhood. I had no idea you were enduring such pain."

My voice trembled as I replied, "Tara, please tell me how I can make you feel better. How can I ease your pain?" I pleaded with her.

"I want you to give me a tight hug, Neil," she said with a tender voice.

I hurried towards her and gently embraced her, pulling her close to my chest. Tears streamed down our faces, but in each other's arms, we found solace. She rested her head on my chest, and I could hear her silent sobs. She was delicate and vulnerable, and I wished to merge with the moment.

In that embrace, we transcended to a different realm.

Suddenly, we heard giggling sounds coming from Kabir and Kayla in the background. I tried to release Tara from the hug, but she resisted, wanting to freeze that moment. I supported her weight so she could stand at ease.

Kabir and Kayla's voices drifted towards us, their affectionate whispers and promises of eternal togetherness in between kisses.

After approximately 15 minutes of the heartfelt embrace, we slowly separated. Tara looked down, wiping away her tears. I cupped her face with both hands, gently lifting her gaze to meet mine. I brushed her hair, held her hand, and kissed her forehead.

Something shifted inside her, and she closed her eyes for a few seconds.

By then, Kabir and Kayla had noticed us. They called out to us from a distance, and we walked towards them. They looked at us, and Kabir asked with a smile, "He's not bothering you again, right Tara?"

She simply smiled in response, and together we all walked back to our suite.

Tara emerged from the washroom, having just taken a shower to wash away the saltiness in the air.

When I returned from the washroom, I found her still engrossed in writing her diary.

I put on my headphones and stepped out onto the balcony. My favorite song was playing on my Spotify playlist- "Tujhse naraz nahi Zindagi...Hairan hu main..."

The next thing I knew, the first rays of the sun hit my face, waking me up. I had fallen asleep on the chair.

I entered the room, and Tara was still asleep. I freshened up and stepped out of the suit.

I walked into the room and found Tara almost ready for breakfast. Her happiness was evident as she greeted me with a pleasant smile, causing my ears to ring,

"Good morning, madam," I said, smiling. "Are we ready to go?"

Tara nodded, and together we embarked on our itinerary for the day. The morning was incredibly beautiful, and I couldn't help but admire Tara's stunning appearance in her pastel-green gown. Her slightly damp hair added to her overall beauty.

As we arrived at our destination, I was mesmerized by the setup that Kabir and Kayla had impeccably prepared. Tables were arranged by the ocean, with a large oval table at the center, capable of seating 25-30 people.

Kabir guided us to this grand table, where Kayla greeted us with a radiant smile and an air of happiness. We took our seats, joined by Kabir's and Kayla's parents, as well as a few bodyguards for added security.

Given Kayla's father's reputation as a minister in the central government and her mother's position as a graceful IFS officer, it was only fitting to have some extra protection.

Kabir's father raised a toast, and laughter filled the air as we all dined together. The moment was filled with pure bliss.

While having breakfast, Tara returned to her charming self, playfully teasing me and Kabir. Seeing her like this brought me immense joy and satisfaction.

Afterward, we decided to take a stroll by the ocean, which Tara fondly referred to as "Her Home." As we walked, I couldn't contain my curiosity and asked Tara enthusiastically, "What do you write in your diary, Tara?"

She chuckled and smiled in response, "The things that I'm afraid to tell others."

I was surprised by her answer, "Is that so?"

With a mischievous smile, she nodded, "Yeahhh...!"

Curiosity piqued, I pressed further, eager to know more. However, Tara remained silent, continuing to walk with a secret smile. Eventually, I couldn't help but urge her for an answer.

Softly, she responded, "One day, I will let you read it."

I scoffed playfully as we continued our pleasant walk. Tara's silent smile suggested she had something on her mind, but I had no clue about it.

Tara asked on our way back, "Shall we go back to the room now?"

I teased her, "So you can write your diary again?"

A shy blush spread across Tara's cheeks, making them even redder.

Smiling, I nodded and gently held her hand, noticing that the bruise was healing. I asked softly,

"Does it still hurt?"

She shook her head negatively and smiled, looking into my eyes.

Upon reaching our suite, as expected, Tara sat down to write her diary, while I opened my laptop to check my emails.

Lost in her thoughts, Tara dozed off on the chair by the window, immersed in her writing. I glanced at her for a moment, smiled, and left the room to find Kabir.

The cocktail party in the evening was highly anticipated. Kabir and Kayla were brimming with excitement, evident from their glowing faces.

Tara, on the other hand, seemed uninterested in attending,

"What will I even do at a cocktail party? I don't even drink."

However, Kayla firmly insisted that she had to join.

I returned to the suite around 4 p.m., reminding myself that we had to leave for the party at 5 p.m.

Upon entering, I noticed Tara struggling with her antique necklace.

Ignoring her struggle for the moment, I grabbed my laptop. Secretly stealing glances at her while working, I admired her silently in her black dress and pink heels. She looked breathtaking.

After a while, she called out, "Neil... would you mind, please?"

She was still struggling with her necklace.

Confused by her request, I thought to myself, "Mind? What is she saying?"

"My mind is not even functioning right now, so it's out of the equation," I chuckled inwardly.

I carefully tucked her long hair away and fixed her necklace, then walked away with a smile, returning to my laptop.

She left the room to join Kayla, while I unintentionally dozed off for about an hour.

Tara returned around 5 p.m., and I woke up to the sound of her footsteps in her heels. Glancing at the time, I realized it was already time to leave for the party. I quickly grabbed my tuxedo and hurried into the bathroom.

As I emerged from the bathroom, she looked at me and suddenly smiled.

Confused, I asked, "What's wrong?"

"Nothing," she giggled mischievously.

"Looks like someone is going to get a lot of proposals today." her smile was contagious.

"Ohh... really... even the one I've been waiting for so long?" I chuckled back mischievously with a hidden excitement in my voice.

She smiled back with an essence of secrecy. After 10 minutes, we made our way to the party hall.

The party was a lively and vibrant affair, filled with laughter, music, and the sound of clinking glasses. As we entered the beautifully decorated venue, we were greeted by the sight of impeccably dressed guests mingling and engrossed in animated conversations.

The room was adorned with stunning floral arrangements, adding a touch of elegance to the atmosphere. Gentle, ambient lighting enveloped the space, creating a warm and inviting ambiance that set the perfect backdrop for the evening.

The soft melodies of a jazz band filled the air from a corner of the room, creating a relaxed and sophisticated vibe that urged everyone to sway and tap their feet to the rhythm.

The waitstaff moved gracefully through the crowd, offering trays of delectable hors d'oeuvres and expertly crafted signature cocktails. The tantalizing aroma of the culinary delights wafted through the room, teasing and tempting everyone's taste buds.

Groups of friends and acquaintances gathered together, engaged in lively conversations, their laughter echoing throughout the space. The energy in the room was infectious, making it easy to strike up conversations with new faces, find common ground, and discover shared interests.

Amidst clinking glasses and occasional bursts of cheers, guests raised their glasses and toasted joyous occasions, successful endeavors, and cherished friendships. The atmosphere was filled with celebrations of life and reasons to revel in happiness.

The glasses sparkled with an array of colorful concoctions, each one meticulously prepared by skilled mixologists. From timeless martinis to inventive and creative blends, the bar became a focal point of the event, generating an air of excitement and anticipation with each sip.

Inside the hall, Tara and I made our way, where we were greeted by Kayla and Kabir. Kayla looked as beautiful as ever, while Kabir exuded charm in his black tuxedo.

They quickly arranged for a waiter to bring us drinks. Kabir, Kayla, and I each picked up our drinks, while Kayla took the waiter aside to explain something. She returned with the news that Tara's mocktail was on its way.

Caught up in the moment, I realized that Tara needed some fresh air in these types of parties. Soon, the waiter arrived with her mocktail. I leaned in and asked, "Would you like to step outside for a while?"

She smiled and nodded as if I had just granted her deepest wish.

We ventured outside, each with our respective drinks in hand. Tara and I found a table nearby and settled down. We engaged in light conversation for a while before deciding to head back inside to the party hall.

We re-entered the party hall, and Kayla approached us, inviting Tara and me to join in the dancing. The music filled the air, and everyone seemed to be swaying and moving with the melodies. Looking around, I saw the joyous atmosphere with everyone on the dance floor.

I reached out my hand to Tara, and her eyes lit up as she came closer to me. I held her by her waist, and her hand rested on my shoulder. We interlocked our other hands. I noticed that she was shaking slightly, "Are you okay?"

Tara nodded softly, and we began to dance together, starting with slow and graceful movements that gradually escalated into swift steps.

A mix of emotions overwhelmed me as Tara was so close, and I felt myself on the verge of freezing from the intensity. After some time, she pressed herself even closer and rested her head on my shoulder, and we continued our dance.

When the music ceased, we gently pulled away from each other. Kayla indicated our table, and we sat down, spending approximately an hour together. Meanwhile, Kabir and Kayla were having their cherished moments, dancing with affection and culminating in a long, beautiful kiss.

Tara appeared different to me at that moment, quieter than usual. After some time, Kayla and Kabir joined us, and we all left the hall together.

Tara seemed to be losing her balance occasionally, but she managed to steady herself somehow. Kayla noticed and pulled me aside, concerned. She confided, "Neil, I think I have made a mistake."

I looked at her in shock, "What do you mean?"

"Please, don't get angry, and don't tell Kabir, but I asked the waiter to mix a little alcohol in Tara's drink. I only intended for her to relax a bit and enjoy the party, but it seems she's not feeling well," Kayla nervously explained.

"What the hell did you do? You know she doesn't drink, right?" I tried to keep my voice low but couldn't hide my astonishment.

"I'm sorry, please help take care of her tonight for me," she pleaded.

As we returned to where Kabir and Tara were standing, I looked at Tara and noticed her eyes reddening. It was clear that she struggled to maintain her balance in her heels.

Addressing everyone, I spoke with concern, "We're going to the room for a while. We need to freshen up, and I think Tara could use some rest."

Kabir and Kayla nodded in agreement, and I held Tara's hand to support her as we made our way. Once we reached the room, Tara remained in silence, unaware of the fact that she had just consumed alcohol for the first time in her life.

I asked her to sit comfortably on the bed, and she leaned against the headrest. Sensing the nervousness in my eyes, Tara questioned, "Everything okay, Neil?"

I nodded, mustered a smile, and maintained my patience, hoping to support her through whatever was to come.

I was interrupted by my phone ringing—it was my mom asking for the details of Kabir's wedding and sharing that she wouldn't be able to join the celebration due to some reasons. Stepping outside onto the balcony, I engaged in a short conversation with her.

After about five minutes, I returned to the room only to find Tara asleep, half-lying on the bed. I approached her, attempting to awaken her, but she remained unresponsive.

Carefully, I adjusted her position on the bed and gently lifted her to place a pillow beneath her head. I covered her with a light quilt, observing her peaceful sleep before turning to retrieve my laptop.

However, as I tried to free my hand from hers, Tara held on tightly and softly murmured my name, "Neil..."

I moved closer to her, but her words were faint and difficult to discern. She was unwilling to release my hand, so I sat down beside her on the bed, resting my back against the wall of the bedrest and caressing her hair. Once again, she uttered, "Neil... Please don't leave me alone. Please don't go."

I remained by her side, unable to bring myself to leave. Time seemed to slip away, and the next thing I knew, I had fallen asleep while sitting, with my back against the bedrest, and Tara continued to sleep, still holding my hand.

When the morning sun illuminated the room, I tried to get up, but my movement stirred Tara from her slumber. Rubbing her eyes, she looked at me sitting beside her, holding her hands, and apologized sincerely,

"Oh My God, Neil... I'm so sorry. I hope I didn't keep you from sleeping."

"Were you here all night?" She was filled with remorse.

Trying to reassure her, I replied, "No need to worry, Tara. You were tired; that's all." I didn't want her to know about the mocktail incident.

"But my head feels heavy, and I've never had this headache before," she almost cried, clearly in discomfort.

I offered her some coffee and suggested that she rest a bit more. We had a lot of leisure time scheduled for the day, as Kayla had prepared individual itineraries for each of us. The timing was flexible, so after the coffee, Tara went back to sleep, and I reclined on the sofa to finally get the much-needed rest I had missed out on.

19

♥Nineteen

I woke up around 10:30 A.M and felt that the couch was soft, but not ideal for someone of my height (5'10"). Tara was already awake, sitting on the balcony and enjoying her coffee. I approached her and greeted her,

"Hey... How are you?"

She responded with a nod and a guilty look on her face.

"Neil, I will ask Kayla if she can arrange a separate room for us. I don't want you to be uncomfortable sleeping here," Tara said softly.

I smiled looking at her, "Who said I'm uncomfortable, Tara? This is one of the most comfortable spots for me in a long time."

Tara returned her attention to her coffee and continued to gaze out at the ocean while writing in her mysterious diary.

Afterward, I made my way back to Kabir, hoping to assist with the arrangements. As I reached the gate, a few waiters approached me with big cartons. Tara and I were both unsure about what it could be.

The waiters explained, "Kayla Madam sent these for you, ma'am."

Tara eagerly opened the boxes, revealing a complete set-up for canvas painting in this beautiful natural setting. It was the next activity on Tara's itinerary, and she had been missing it since returning from Mumbai.

She jumped up happily and hugged me,

"Oh my God, look Neil... She is amazing."

Caught off guard by the hug, I managed to adjust and handle both of us. At that moment, I was no longer upset with Kayla, as she had brought a smile and light back into Tara's eyes. Tara seemed a little shy as she realized the situation, her cheeks turning redder and her eyes widening.

She pulled back from the hug and immediately began unpacking the set-up. I helped her, and as per her request, I fixed the canvas set up on the balcony next to her chair. Tara busied herself with her color palettes, creating something with great focus.

Before leaving for Kabir, I caught myself staring at her for a while, captivated by her presence. Upon reaching Kabir, who was giving instructions to the waiters for decorations, he saw me and smiled.

"How is Tara now? Kayla felt so guilty that she told me everything yesterday," he asked.

I nodded gently and replied, "She's better now, and Kayla's canvas set-up has completely healed her."

Kabir patted my shoulder and looked into my eyes. Curiously, he asked, "Did you two talk?"

Confused, I responded, "About what?"

"That you're in love with her. And from what I can see, she feels the same way for you," Kabir said, smiling.

"Bro, let's plan your wedding here. There's not much else going on in my heart," I replied sarcastically.

"The whole world can see the love in your eyes for her, Neil. You can hide everything else, but your eyes have always been the most expressive ever." Kabir said.

I looked down and then made eye contact with him, responding with a gentle smile. He added, "Bhai, don't torture yourself. She deserves to know."

I walked away with a smile, leaving Kabir to deal with the waiters and preparations.

I made my way to the ocean, walking right into the water until I reached the spot where Tara had been the other day. Each wave that struck me brought a sense of relief and trust.

The waves touched my waist and brushed against my hands from time to time. I stayed there for a while before taking a few steps back. I found a table nearby and sat down, resting my head against the back of the chair.

From where I sat, I could see our balcony where Tara was working on her canvas. She seemed completely lost in the ambiance around her. After a while, I took out my phone and started scrolling, trying to enjoy the relaxing vibe.

Noon came, and the sun beamed down on my forehead. It was getting too hot, so I decided to leave the place and head to the gym. I had missed it a lot. I worked out hard for about an hour and then sat in the lounge to cool off for a bit.

After a few minutes, Kayla messaged me, "You have a package at the reception. Go and promise me that you won't open it until I tell you to. And please, keep it hidden from everyone."

"What?" I asked curiously.

"Promise me, Neil, that you won't open the package until I ask you to. And keep it a secret," she typed again

"Okay, as you say," I shrugged and made my way to the reception.

There, a young man approached me and said, "Mr. Neil Wadia, I have something for you." He handed me a small black bag that was tightly packed with something inside.

I wondered what it could be, but as I had promised Kayla, I didn't open it. Instead, I went back to my room to keep it safely hidden.

Tara was still painting, and although I couldn't see what she was working on due to the view being blocked, I could tell she was happy doing it.

I ordered lunch for both of us and quickly headed to the bathroom to take a shower as soon as possible.

I returned to find Tara still engrossed in her color palettes. We exchanged glances and shared smiles.

The food had arrived by now, so we sat down together to eat before it got cold. Tara's eyes were still red, and her messy hair only added to her beauty.

After finishing our lunch, Tara went back to her canvas, while I decided to take a short nap.

When I woke up later in the evening, Tara was still painting. The backdrop of the red sky made her look like a divine angel.

Night had already fallen, and we headed for dinner by the ocean. After a long walk, we returned to our suite.

Tomorrow was going to be a long day, with the Haldi ceremony scheduled. Everyone was instructed to wear yellow.

As I returned from the washroom, Tara hesitatingly suggested,

"Neil, I think we can share this big bed. We're not kids anymore. Don't worry, I won't attack you or anything. We can keep a few pillows boundary between us just in case you're scared." She chuckled softly till the end of her sentence.

I smiled at her invitation, thinking to myself, "Tara, if I'm ever going to share a bed with you for the first time, there won't be any boundaries." I looked down and smiled at my thoughts.

She was still waiting for my response, to which I finally said, "Tara, I'm fine here. Don't worry about me." I assured her and went to sleep on the couch.

20

♥Twenty

On a radiant and sunny day, we had to join Kabir and Kayla's Haldi celebration venue at noon.

I woke up early around 7 a.m. and decided to hit the gym. Tara was still fast asleep, and I didn't want to disturb her peaceful slumber.

After an intense workout session that lasted around 90 minutes, I returned to the room to find Tara engrossed in writing something in her diary. When she glanced up at me, I was soaked in sweat, evidence of the rigorous exercise. We exchanged smiles, and she went back to her diary.

Feeling hungry, I ordered some breakfast and quickly freshened up in the washroom. When I returned, wearing a light yellow kurta paired with denim, Tara looked at me and offered a small smile before devoting herself to her writing once again.

We made our way to the breakfast table, where I convinced Tara to join me. We enjoyed a delicious meal while basking in the ocean air, teasing and laughing together.

At one point, Tara stood up and asked me to close my eyes. She took my hand and led me to the balcony. Determined not to peek before the appointed time, I waited anxiously.

Finally, Tara instructed me to open my eyes, revealing a stunning canvas in front of me. It was filled with vibrant colors and overflowing with love. I was rendered speechless by its beauty. Tara had poured her heart into creating this masterpiece. She finally asked,

"Do you like it?"

I gazed at her, unable to contain my emotions, and blinked my eyes with a soft smile on my lips. Finally, I said, "This is the most beautiful thing I have ever seen, Tara."

The canvas depicted a couple dancing in the moonlit ocean. Their closeness and the way they embraced each other reverberated with a divine connection.

I held Tara's hand, unable to resist planting a kiss on the back of her fingers. She gracefully smiled and said, "I'm glad you liked it, Neil."

Suddenly, she remembered, "Oh my god, I need to get ready! Kayla will be furious if we're late."

She playfully pulled her hand away and hurried to the washroom. I also walked out of the room to meet up with Kabir.

When I reached the Haldi setup, I was greeted by a stunning sight. The entire venue was adorned with colorful decorations, creating an atmosphere of celebration.

Marigold flowers, known for their vibrant yellow color, were prominently used in the decor. Strings of marigold garlands adorned the entrance, radiating a warm and inviting ambiance.

The seating arrangements for the guests were arranged in a circular pattern, allowing everyone to have a clear view of the ceremony. Colorful cushions and low seating options were provided, adding to the relaxed and intimate atmosphere of the occasion.

In the center of the venue, a beautifully decorated canopy was set up, draping in flowing yellow fabrics and adorned with marigold blooms. This was the focal point of the ceremony, where Kabir and Kayla would be seated for the haldi application.

A small stage was also set up nearby, hosting traditional musicians who played lively folk tunes, adding to the festive spirit. The rhythmic beats of the drums and the melodious notes of the flute filled the air, creating an uplifting and celebratory ambiance.

Baskets filled with turmeric paste, sandalwood powder, and other traditional haldi ingredients were placed strategically around the ceremony area. These would be used by family and friends to apply the haldi paste on Kabir and Kayla, symbolizing the blessings and well wishes for their upcoming union.

I took some pictures as the setup for the event was nearly complete. Everyone gathered around, including Kabir and Kayla, who entered hand in hand with smiles on their faces.

I was waiting for Tara to join us, but there was no sign of her yet. Kayla, wearing a soft yellow lehenga and beautiful floral jewelry, approached me and asked, "Where is Tara?"

I replied, "She's getting ready. She'll be here soon."

After waiting for about 30 minutes, Tara still hadn't arrived. I called her, but there was no response.

I went to the room and opened the door to find Tara not yet dressed, but writing in her diary. I felt myself becoming agitated, and I exclaimed,

"Tara, Kayla is upset outside. Everyone is waiting for you."

She nodded, saying, "Just a second, Neil."

I couldn't resist the temptation any longer. Something overcame me, and I gently took the diary from her hands,

"Today, I'm going to solve this mystery, Tara."

She jumped up from her seat, trying to grab the diary back, pleading, "Please, Neil, you can't read it, at least not yet. Please give it back."

I moved around the room, holding the diary, finally managing to leave the room.

Now, I was filled with curiosity to know what had been keeping Tara so occupied since we arrived. She kept calling my name from the door but I didn't respond. I wanted to read the diary first.

I walked towards the ocean, the noon sun shining brightly overhead. Finding some shade, I settled on the sand and opened it to read.

"I can't comprehend how God could be so kind, sending you into my life when I needed you the most. The way you look at me makes me feel more secure than ever before. Every moment spent with you is filled with warmth and coziness, creating a new haven of happiness for me.

Our little Pani puri dates and coffee chitchats have spoiled me to the point where I can't imagine a life without you. The intimate dinner we shared at my home felt so comforting that I could happily eat the same meal for the rest of my life as long as you were sitting next to me.

The dance we shared that night evoked a sense of serenity in me that I wish to hold onto forever by holding your hands.

Watching the strands of your hair fall gently onto your forehead while you work on your laptop makes me long to give you a tender kiss on that very spot.

When you took care of me when I was sick, simply holding your hand was enough for me. I wished to freeze that moment and relish in your presence, which feels like a symphony of melodies surrounding me.

On the day you were angry with me, I could not forgive myself for what happened, and perhaps I never will be able to. The mere thought of someone demeaning you fills me with despair.

The day you came to my office, looking deeply into my eyes, and asked, 'What about us, Tara?' felt like a moment I wanted to hold onto forever and never let you go. I could never stay angry at you; instead, I was angry at myself for not fully grasping your thoughts and emotions.

I want to return to Mumbai so I can ensure that I never hurt you again, although I know I will always miss you there too. Every second spent with you feels like absolute bliss to me.

Each time you hold my hand and gently caress the bruise on it, I yearn to embrace you, Neil. A hug that would last an eternity because it's incredibly difficult for me to be apart from you. You might find it silly, but I never wanted that bruise to heal. I didn't want to lose the comfort of your touch.

Your tender eyes hold a mysterious feeling that often leaves me confused and afraid that I might not fully understand them and unintentionally cause you pain like I did before.

The cocktail night party and the way you protected and cared for me have stirred something deep within me. In truth, Kayla revealed everything in a letter she sent me along with the canvas setup."

The way you hug me, and embrace me, Neil, makes me melt in your strong arms. I just get no control over me. Your tenderness and care towards others are going to make you so successful in your life.

I L..."

"I closed my eyes, and tears rolled down my cheeks as I put the diary aside and got lost in thought. Her words, emotions, and vulnerability filled my mind, overwhelming me with feelings. My body shook with my heart racing faster, and I felt breathless even in the fresh air.

Hoping to find Tara, I rushed to the setup. As soon as I arrived, Kabir and Kayla almost shouted, 'Where the hell have you been?' I smiled and looked up at Tara, who was nervous, and anxious, but still effortlessly carrying a beautiful yellow saree.

Our eyes met briefly, and I could feel her trembling. Telling Kabir and Kayla to return later, I leaned towards Tara and whispered in her ear, 'Come with me, Please!' Holding her hand, we walked away, only to be hit by a big splash of yellow water mixed with flower petals, turning us into a colorful mess.

Holding Tara's hand firmly, I headed toward the suite. The 100 miles felt like an eternity. Once we entered the suit, I closed the door behind us. We were both covered in haldi and flower petals from head to toe, and I could feel her shaking hand in mine as I pulled her to the bathroom.

As we reached the walk-in shower, I held Tara tightly by her waist, pushing her against the wall as we stood beneath the shower, water pouring over our heads. Our clothes were already wet and stained with Haldi, but the color and petals washed away, flowing beneath our feet. Tara looked down at my feet, shivering from head to toe. Finally, I spoke with a soft voice:

"How could you, Tara? Look at me...Please."

She met my gaze for a moment before reluctantly turning away again. Her pink eyes conveyed her guilt; she had been crying for some time. I came closer to her to prevent the water from flowing over her head; our silent eyes spoke a thousand words. I repeated,

"How could you do this to me, Tara?"

I held her close, my breath warming her chin. I could feel her nervousness.

"How could you hide such a big pile of emotions from me?" I asked, my voice trembling.

She finally spoke,

"I'm sorry... I..."

The water flowed as we stood together in the shower, and I felt her heartbeat against my chest.

I intervened with her,

"Not sure? Really? How could you be so clueless, Tara? The whole world could read my eyes, but how could you not? Why didn't you say anything?"

She whispered back,

"You also didn't say anything, Neil..."

I pulled her tightly, and whispered to her more closely,

"Trust me Tara I wanted to...Was about to ... remember the bonfire eve..?"

She nodded, she was continuously shivering, I turned off the shower.

I continued with a soft voice,

"But I got scared. Knowing how deeply I have hurt you. I was not worthy of your affection or trust. M sorry babyyy."

At last word, she trembled and closed her eyes, her lips were a little apart, but she could manage to say,

“You can never hurt me, Neil.”

I wrapped my fingers around her waist, her saree was soaked with water, our skin was in direct touch, and with each touch, she was shuddering.

“Did u read it in full...?It was not complete, Neil, You pulled it in the middle when I was writing” she wobbled.

I pressed her hand gently,

"I have read it enough, I want to hear you here at this moment."

I playfully caressed her hair falling on her face. As I approached her closer, She looked over her shoulder, I planted a kiss on the side of her neck. She almost got fumbled.

She was Shivering with the water dripping from my body over hers,

"Neil...please.....I....”

I planted one more kiss on her cheek, low enough to touch the corners of her lips. She had lost control of her body. Her breath came in ragged gasps, and each one I could count. Her warm breath fell on my lips, I could feel it all over me.

My body was totally over hers now, pressing against her from shoulder to thigh against the wall behind her.

I gently leaned in close to her, my lips grazing her delicate earlobe as I whispered breathlessly, “ Tara, I am all yours..."

In that moment, she embraced me with such fervor, as if she wanted to dissolve into my very being. I tenderly wrapped my arms around her, yearning to hear the tender words that hung in the air.

With her eyes closed, a single tear escaped, tracing its path down her flushed cheek. And then, with a vulnerability that consumed my soul, she uttered those three magical words,

"I love you, Neil."

The sound of her confession reverberated through me, leaving me trembling in awe. It was as if time stood still, and without hesitation, my lips naturally found hers, lightly caressing her soft, pink petals.

I held her close, steadying her as the world spun around us, our kiss deepening with each passing second, a fervent declaration of our love.

But as fate would have it, our moment of bliss was interrupted by the persistent ring of my phone, breaking the spell that had enveloped us. Tara quickly composed herself, tender and bashful, as she adjusted her saree.

Reluctantly, I released my hold on her, whispering promises of my return. Stepping out of the washroom,

It was Kabir, "I need you urgently here."

With a quick adjustment of my appearance and a change of clothes, I prepared to step back into the outside world, leaving Tara behind as she stayed back in the washroom to take a shower.

Before leaving, I left her a tender message, "Will be back soon, Tara, Love you."

21

♥Twenty-One

I was looking for Kabir when Kayla found me.

“Hey, how’s Tara, Where is she? Is everything okay?” Kayla was curious.

I nodded softly in return which gave her a sigh of relief.

“Okay listen, it’s time to open that packet that I gave you. And always keep it with you till I give further instructions” she ordered

A lot of questions were flooding from her side, and I just could smile when Kabir came to approach me.

“Bhai, What happened? You were looking so damn anxious and left with Tara without saying anything. Is she okay? Is everything okay? He was anxious.

I reassured him and patted his back.

I whispered something in his ear, causing him to jump up and exclaim, "What???? Bhai...congratulations!"

He hugged me tightly, still jumping with joy, and said, "It's done, it will be ready."

My heart was filled with a rhythm of pure happiness that no one could match.

I was about to leave to see Tara when Kabir's dad stopped me,

"Beta, have you seen Kabir? I have a long list of tasks to complete, but I can't find him anywhere. The wedding planner had an emergency and had to leave. Tomorrow is the big Mehendi and Sangeet event. Neil, could you please help me with the list?"

"Sure, Uncle, please tell me," I smiled.

He explained the tasks that needed to be completed, and I got to work to finish them on time. It was a challenging job with multiple workers around. As I neared completion, I checked the time and realized it was already 2 a.m. The constant visits to the markets and vendors had left me exhausted, and I had lost track of time.

Once the setup was done, I made my way to find Tara. It had been a whole day without any contact with her, and I longed to see her badly.

When I entered the room, Tara was fast asleep.

I quickly and silently freshened up by washing my face before returning to my couch. It had been an incredibly tiring and busy day, and I immediately dozed off.

The next morning, I felt a gentle touch on my hands. I rubbed my eyes, Tara was sitting near me, holding my hands.

She whispered, "Good morning."

I smiled, sat up, and hugged her tightly, "Good morning, baby."

She took deep breaths as if trying to absorb my scent into herself,

"I missed you, Neil."

I kissed her softly on her cheeks, and she blushed shyly. I gently caressed her hair, which had fallen messily onto her face.

I ordered breakfast, and we had it together.

I checked my phone, Kabir's dad had messaged me," Beta please join me ASAP."

I took a quick shower and asked Tara to get ready for the day.

I left the suit and found my way to Kabir's Dad. I started again with the final preparations and arrangements.

Kabir and Kayla were about to have a big day today.

It was almost noon. I glanced at the clock, it was already 4 PM I rushed towards the suit as everybody was gathering around for the celebration.

I entered the room, but Tara was not there. I checked my phone, and she had dropped a message, "Heading to Kayla's room. See you at the event."

I called Kabir inquiring about something, and he assured me,

"Everything will be arranged as you told Bhai, Don't worry."

When I got ready, everybody was instructed to wear green. I put on a green kurta with off-white pajamas. I headed towards Kayla's room to meet the love of my life,' Tara'.

I knocked on Kayla's room, She was getting ready, and I could hear the giggling of her friends inside. I called Tara to meet me outside.

After about 5 minutes, she came and I just kept staring at her. My eyes were frozen at the moment. She was looking extremely beautiful. My heart almost stopped breathing. She was carrying a green silk lehenga. Her open hair added grace to her attire, Her neck was covered with a heavy necklace, and was wearing big earrings. My eyes got stuck on his forehead which was radiating with a small 'bindi' and a 'Maang tika'.

She was feeling shy seeing me staring at her. I came closer to her, wrapped my hand around her waist, and walked with her. She was quiet and silently walking with me.

We reached the venue of the celebration. Kayla pulled her from my hand for the mehendi application on her hands. She smiled at me and walked with her.

I was watching her and was feeling on top of the world. Dhol music and melodies were ringing in my ears. Everyone was enjoying, laughing, and celebrating together.

I was still watching Tara surrounded by mehendi artists. She seemed so happy that it was beyond description.

The Sangeet was ready and everyone was performing and showering their blessings to the soon-to-be married couple.

Once Tara finished with her mehendi, she approached me with a bright smile and a chuckle. Her hands looked incredibly beautiful, and her happiness was palpable.

I noticed that her hair kept touching her lips, so I gently pulled them back. Just then, the other girls dragged Tara to the stage where she danced with full enthusiasm, enjoying the song "Mehndi laga ke rakhna...Doli saja ke rakhna..."

From a distance, I watched her graceful movements and admired her. Kabir approached me and said,

"Bro, the work is done. All the best!"

I nodded in acknowledgment and patiently continued watching Tara on the stage.

At that moment, I received a message from Kayla, instructing me to open a box that I would need today.

Tara finished her performance and stepped off the stage, she was trying to catch her breath. I held her closely, helping her regain her balance. I leaned towards her and whispered, "Come with me, please."

She looked at me with silent curiosity. With reassuring looks, I held her waist and guided her towards the darkened surroundings. We could barely see the moonlight touching our skin.

As we reached the ocean, Tara's expression shifted to one of happiness, and she looked at me with a warm smile. I pulled her closer and led her into the water. The waves gently lapping against our hands, and our clothes were already soaked up to our waist. We continued moving further into the ocean until we reached a certain point.

Turning towards Tara, I kissed her forehead, surprising her. Her eyes reflected love and nervousness.

I went down on one knee, holding a ring that had been sent by Kayla in the packet.

Tears filled Tara's eyes, with a few of them rolling down her cheeks. At that moment, we noticed a beautifully lit setup at a short distance. It included the canvas made by Tara, a guitar, and numerous roses forming the words,

"I LOVE YOU."

A song played in the background,

"Aap Ki nazron ne samjha...Peyaar ke kabil mujhe..." It was Kabir who had prepared the entire setup at my request.

Softly, I held her hands and asked,

"TARA PATEL, WILL YOU MARRY ME?"

Sitting in the ocean, where the waves washed over me, Tara sat down beside me, embracing me tightly. She uttered the words,

"YESSSSSS......"

I slipped the ring onto her finger, and she was still teary-eyed with emotions. Standing up together, our lips brushed against each other, we shared a heartfelt kiss. The music continued playing, so I asked Tara for a dance.

She chuckled and asked,

"What?.. In the ocean?"

I smiled looking at her,

"That's exactly what we're doing on your canvas, right?"

Locking eyes, I pulled her closer, and together we danced in the ocean. The cold water embraced us intermittently as we moved to the rhythm of our steps, completely lost in the moment.

Later, we made our way towards the beautifully lit setup on the sandy beach. With water dripping all around us, Tara and I sat down on the cold sand. Her head was over my shoulder. I picked up the guitar singing softly,

"Teraaaaa... hone lagaaaaa hooooon....!"

www.ingramcontent.com/pod-product-compliance
Lightning Source LLC
LaVergne TN
LVHW091055150826
845673LV00002B/588